It's a Girl Thing

Books in the Holly's Heart series

It's a Girl Thing

BEVERLY ♥ LEWIS

ZondervanPublishingHouse
Grand Rapids, Michigan

A Division of HarperCollinsPublishers

It's a Girl Thing
Copyright © 1997 by Beverly Lewis

Requests for information should be addressed to:

ZondervanPublishingHouse
Grand Rapids, Michigan 49530

Library of Congress Cataloging-in-Publication Data
Lewis, Beverly, 1949–.
   It's a girl thing / Beverly Lewis.
      p.   cm. — (Holly's heart ; [bk. 14]))
   Summary: Fifteen-year-old Holly is all set to go to Washington D.C.
with her school choir over spring break, but she fears the timing might
conflict with the birth of her mother and stepfather's new baby.
   ISBN: 0-310-20845-9 (softcover)
   [1. Stepfamilies—Fiction.   2. High schools—Fiction.   3. Schools—
Fiction.   4. Christian Life—Fiction.]   I. Title.   II. Series: Lewis,
Beverly, 1949–   Holly's heart series ; [bk. 14].
PZ7.L58464It   k1997
[Fic]–dc21   97-2142
                                                                       CIP
                                                                        AC

Printed in the United States of America

97 98 99 00 01 02 03 04 /❖ DH/ 10 9 8 7 6 5 4 3 2 1

For
my delightful fans
in Topeka, Kansas—
Mindy and Katie Dow

❤ Author's Note ❤

When I was young, my mother used to say, "All good things must come to an end," and I wondered why that had to be. But in the case of the Holly's Heart series, it's understandable that fourteen books make a solid series. Some of you may not agree, but I thank you for your fantastic support and ongoing encouragement for my work, as well as your exuberance for the series.

I do hope you've discovered my SummerHill Secrets books for girls, filled with suspense, adventure, and yes, a touch of romance, as well as my novel, *The Shunning*, the first of an adult trilogy.

So, as you see, we'll continue to journey together, you and I, perhaps in settings far removed from Holly's beloved Dressel Hills, perhaps not, but there will always be more endearing characters to laugh and cry with, because that's the way my story people simply must be—as true-to-life as possible—for you, my dear reader.

Special thanks goes to my daughter Julie Marie and her girlfriends, Julie and Cindy Hauk, who helped concoct the main plot for this book. And to Amy Birch, my niece, who accidentally, yet illegally, took a flash picture inside the Bureau of Engraving and Printing in Washington, D.C.!

O N E

Opening my eyes, I sat up in bed and stretched. A fabulous sensation zipped through me, something like the adrenaline rush you get when you know beyond any doubt that something incredible is about to happen. I could feel the excitement in my bones—wrapped right around my nerve endings.

Hours later at school, I stopped at Andrea Martinez's locker to tell her about my jazzed feeling. Andie reacted a bit nonchalantly, and I should've expected as much. My best friend's not a morning person. Who is?

Anyway, she got bossy on me. "Take a deep breath, girl. You'll get over it."

"But you know how it is, when there's anticipation electrifying the air?" I said.

Andie shrugged and touched her short, dark

curls, obviously not wildly interested. "Maybe you've got it in your mind that we placed at district choir auditions. But don't go getting your hopes up about Washington, D.C. Lots of choral groups make it this far."

She was right. Still, I couldn't help the feeling . . . and the hoping, holding out for the top prize: a trip to our nation's capital. What a way to top off our freshman year!

If the Dressel Hills High School Show Choir made state finals—and we would find out this week—and then went on to place at regionals, the way I figured it, we'd have a fabulous chance at nationals. And after that, maybe the international choir competitions in Europe!

Andie took her time gathering up her usual Monday morning assortment of books and a three-ring binder for morning classes. I waited for her, trying to control the thrill bumps I felt prancing up my spine. Regionals . . . this Friday!

When her book bag was finally stashed full, the homeroom bell rang. I said my overly enthusiastic good-byes. "See ya second hour," I called over my shoulder before merging with the student congestion. Second hour was choir.

Andie nodded and headed in the opposite direction toward Miss Shaw's homeroom, Room 210. I still found it hard to accept our homeroom setup; Andie and I were in different rooms. Here it was the middle of March, nearly halfway through the second semester of my freshman year. By now I should've been accustomed to separate homerooms. But Andie and I had never really been split up before.

She had, of course, handled the situation well—actually was very cool about it. I was the one having to adapt.

Amy-Liz Thompson, a friend from our church youth group, fell into step with me, and we allowed ourselves to be carried along with the throng of Dressel Hills High School students.

"It's a good thing I'm not as short as Andie," she shouted over the roar. Her wavy honey-blonde hair floated along away from her face. "I'd sink and drown for sure."

"No kidding." That's when I grabbed her elbow and pulled her out of the current. Exit: Room 202.

Jared Wilkins showed up all smiles just as we made the turn into Mr. Irving's homeroom. I heard Amy-Liz groan softly, and she promptly followed me, sliding into the desk ahead of mine.

"Don't worry about Jared," I whispered. "I think he's starting to grow up."

"If you say so." She pulled a notebook out of her book bag. I figured she didn't believe me.

Just then, Stan, my ornery brousin (cousin-turned-stepbrother) poked his head into the room, motioning to me. "Holly," he called softly.

"What's this about," I muttered, getting out of my seat and going to the doorway.

Stan was a sophomore, a bit tall for his age, and almost as blonde as I was. But he had an ever-growing chip on his shoulder, and I wondered how long it would be before it exhibited itself today.

"Look, Holly, I need you to go straight home after school." His voice sounded confident and sure. Like I was going to fall for whatever he said.

"Why should I?"

"Don't ask, just do it," he shot back.

I sighed. This was what I meant about the shoulder chip. He was sixteen now, and the oldest of our blended family. More than anything, he liked to throw his weight around. Especially with me. And it wasn't just my imagination, either. Even Andie and some of my other friends had noticed how Stan seemed to enjoy picking on me.

"I suppose you want me to cover for you," I retorted. "Mom's counting on *you* today, isn't she?"

"C'mon, Holly, just this once." He wasn't asking or pleading. Nope. He was plain cocky.

"So something's come up, right?" I said, his attitude making me upset. "You need me to help out."

His eyebrows floated to his forehead, accompanied by a frown. "Why do you have to be so difficult all the time?" I knew right then that he did not want me to view the situation as a problem that only I could solve for him. He glanced around, probably hoping he wasn't causing a scene.

I sighed. "All the time, huh? Well, thanks for that enlightening comment." I was not going to allow Stan to talk to me this way, not here, at the entrance to my homeroom—a place that was supposed to be a sanctuary, a place secure even from haughty step-brothers. "You came here, wanting a favor, and this is how you act? Well, forget it!" I turned on my heels and marched away—back to my seat and Amy-Liz's curious expression.

"He's totally impossible," I said when I was seated.

"Brothers can be," Amy-Liz replied.

I grinned. My friend was the lucky one. She had no male siblings to drive her crazy. No siblings at all. "What do *you* know about brothers?"

"You're always complaining about yours, that's what!" Amy laughed, but I could see she was dead serious.

"I am?"

Amy shook her head. "As a matter of fact, you complain about Stan a lot. I actually get the feeling that you can't stand him."

"Can't stand Stan," I whispered, trying not to laugh. I thought about it, and was ready to say something back—something to defend my position—but Mr. Irving came in.

I had to settle down and switch my thought mode to academia. It was time for morning announcements even though I had zillions more pertinent comments for Amy-Liz—things to verify the fact that Stan Patterson was *so* a rotten brousin.

TWO

I never had the chance to give Amy-Liz the ear-ful I intended. My government class notes some-how got misplaced, and by the time I located them in my binder and frantically reviewed them for a quiz, it was time for first hour.

The government quiz was child's play, but the homework assignment looked like a nightmare in the making. I jotted down the notes, hoping there wouldn't be tons of this sort of homework dished out all day. It was only first hour, for pete's sake!

After government, I hurried to choir, hoping that we'd have audition results from Mrs. Duncan, our choir director. She made her cheerful entrance, and my hopes soared.

Her stylish, burlap shoulder bag was brimful, as was usually the case. She promptly headed to the piano and began discussing several musical scores with Andie, our accompanist.

It seemed to me that Andie was eager to get to work, because I noticed her fingers wiggling on the piano bench on either side of her. But she listened intently as Mrs. Duncan pointed out various musical phrases. Andie had been doing some radical improvisation at the piano, somewhat hamming it up for the class, while we'd waited for our teacher to show up. Now, though, Andie was focused. And surely as anxious as all of us to know the outcome from district auditions.

I fidgeted, sitting next to Paula and Kayla Miller, my twin girlfriends. "I'm dying to know if we made it," I whispered to Paula.

She nodded. "I certainly hope we did. We sounded absolutely wonderful, didn't you think so?"

"I guess it's hard to tell for sure if you're not out in the audience observing," I said.

Kayla pulled out her compact and peeked at the tiny mirror. "Mrs. Duncan wants to go to Europe as much as the rest of us," she said.

I grinned. Did we really have a chance?

The quiet click of Kayla's compact seemed to signal the end of the director's discussion with Andie. Mrs. Duncan, wearing a navy pantsuit, walked purposefully to the music stand, adjusted it for the correct height, and took the podium.

For a moment, she surveyed each of the choral sections: soprano, alto, tenor, and bass. Then, with a broad smile, she told us the audition results. "Are all of you ready to perform ... again?" Her hands gripped the sides of the music stand.

"Yes!" we cheered.

"All right, then we have some work to do." She gave Andie a nod and raised her hands, and with a gentle sweep of her right hand, we stood in unison. Ready to practice our pieces from memory.

I was almost too giddy to sing. We were actually going to Denver to state auditions!

Partway through the first madrigal, I stepped forward—slightly out of my row—and grinned at Jared Wilkins and Danny Myers just to the right of me, in the boys' section. Jared gave me a not-so-subtle thumbs-up, and Danny, standing next to him, beamed back at me.

Quickly, I turned my attention to Mrs. Duncan's directing, even though I was pretty sure I could sing the entire choral repertoire in my sleep.

❤   ❤   ❤

As it turned out, I did go straight home after school, not so much to help Stan out. I wanted to write a letter to Sean Hamilton, my friend in California.

I'd met Sean, who was a high school junior, two Christmases ago, while visiting my dad and step-mom. During the course of many months of correspondence, he had become quite a close friend. In fact, if I dared to admit it to myself, I really liked Sean. Even more than Jared Wilkins, who had been my very first major crush. Actually, more than any boy I'd ever known.

Sean had a sensible way about him that most younger guys seemed to lack. He was a reliable true friend, and a strong Christian who had agreed to pray with me (long-distance) on several occasions. And he loved kids—maybe because he was already an uncle.

But there was more between us than just friendship, I was beginning to discover. For instance, when he signed off that he missed me or asked when I was coming again to visit my father—those sort of words made my heart flip-flop. And two weeks ago, when Sean called and we'd talked for nearly twenty minutes, I found myself floundering a bit, almost at a loss for words, which never happens!

Mom was okay with his phoning me; she figured we had a good, firm friendship through letters, so it wasn't like I had a serious boyfriend or anything. And she was right. Besides, I was fifteen now—fifteen years and one month old, as of Valentine's Day. That's why I had the unique nickname, Holly-Heart.

Anyway, I couldn't wait to write Sean about our choir winning at districts.

Monday, March 18th

Dear Sean,

I'm so excited! Remember I told you about some of the choral music we were practicing, trying to memorize and polish the songs in time for district auditions?

Well, guess what? We'll be going to Denver this Friday afternoon for state auditions. That's right—we took first place at districts. Can you believe it? (I hardly can myself!) If we make it at state, Mrs. Duncan thinks we have a good chance at regionals, which will be held in Topeka, Kansas. Ever been there?

I went on to tell him about some of the baby-related plans my family had been making. Mom was getting more and more eager as the weeks rolled by and quite uncomfortable, as well. Baby April—we knew it was a girl because of the ultra-sound—was due April 25.

The crib and chest of drawers fits perfectly in my bedroom, which is a large room to begin with. I don't know when I've been so excited about something, unless maybe show choir and the auditions coming up. Of course, that'll only last a short time. Little April will be my sister forever!

I'll write as soon as I know if we place this time. Okay?

Sorry this is so short, but I have gobs of government homework—mostly reading and answering essay-type questions. How about you? Is second semester going well? I hope so.

Write soon.
Your friend,
Holly

P.S. How's your calculus teacher doing now that his chemotherapy is finished? Is his hair growing back yet? Is yours?

Last October, Sean and a bunch of the guys in his class had joined ranks to offer support for their teacher. They'd actually shaved their heads!

As far as I was concerned, it was a noble thing to do. But that was the kind of guy Sean Hamilton was. Maybe that's why I liked him.

♥   ♥   ♥

By the time Stan got home, I'd almost forgotten how bossy he'd been at school. Besides, this was one of the quieter afternoons in the Meredith-Patterson household. Carrie and Stephie hung out in their shared bedroom, listening to a favorite CD, while Phil and Mark did homework on the dining-room table. Surprisingly enough, everything was under control.

Mom, however, would want an explanation from Stan as to why he'd transferred sibling power to me, while she was away from the house.

"You better tell her," I said later. "If she finds out, you'll be in big trouble."

Stan swaggered around the kitchen, searching the cupboards for snack food. "Let me handle it," he muttered.

I figured Stan would probably forget about it, hoping Mom wouldn't find out. He was like that sometimes, irresponsible about the truth.

"I think you better get used to hanging out here after school," I told him. "Our baby sister's gonna need lots of attention."

He snorted. "Don't look at me. I'm not changing diapers—none of that stuff."

What a macho guy he thought he was. "Having a baby around might do you some good," I replied.

"It's a girl thing," he shot back. "And don't forget it!"

"Well, I can see you'll make a fabulous father someday." It was a retaliatory remark, and I could tell by his face that he recognized it as such. Fuel for the fire.

Stan snatched up a large box of pretzels, wearing a determined frown. He marched to the door leading to the family room downstairs. This was not to be the end of round one. Not even close.

THREE

After supper, Mom was settling into her comfortable Boston rocker when Stan sauntered into the living room. He glanced at me, his head doing its jerky number toward the kitchen—my cue to get lost.

As I left the room, I heard him begin to tell Mom about an unexpected intramural game that had come up after school. I was curious to know if he'd get in trouble, so I hung around the area between the dining room and the kitchen, listening.

Uncle Jack came downstairs about then, headed to the living room, and sat down on the couch near Mom. I could see the three of them from my vantage point and was about to indulge myself in a bit of delicious eavesdropping, when Carrie caught me.

"What's going on?" she whispered.

"Nothing."

She scowled. "C'mon, I'm old enough to know things."

"You're only ten," I replied.

"That's almost a teenager." Her eyes flashed impertinence. "So . . . what's Stan in trouble about?"

I wasn't going to let my mouthy little sister blow her top at me. Turning away, I headed downstairs to the family room, where Stephie and the boys were channel surfing in front of the TV.

Carrie followed. "It's about you coming home and baby-sitting us instead of Stan, isn't it?"

My lips were sealed. How did she always seem to know?

"Why aren't you talking to me?" she demanded.

I turned and looked at my one-and-only birth sibling. "You don't get it, do you? I just told you it's none of your business. You're acting like a spoiled brat."

"I'm not a brat—I'm a preteen! Start showing some respect."

I shook my head. "You're hopeless."

"She sure is!" Mark hollered.

"No, she's not!" loyal Stephie shouted back.

And before I could stop it, a full-blown shouting match was under way.

Uncle Jack called down the steps, and when the noise continued, he showed up, looking peeved. "Your mother and I are trying to have a quiet conversation upstairs," he said calmly. "Do you think it might be possible to watch TV without raising the roof?" He smiled unexpectedly. "Very soon, there's going to be a baby in this house, and the five of you"—and here he included me—"may need to rethink your interactive skills."

"It's not my fault," I spoke up.

"You're the oldest in the room, Holly." That's all he said before turning to leave, as though my age made me in charge.

Carrie moved her lips at me, mimicking our step-dad's words, and I charged at her.

"Help!" she yelled. "Holly's gonna—"

I mashed my hand over her mouth. And then I felt it. Her tongue, warm and wet, pushed through her lips into my hand.

"Eew!" I yelled, jumping away. "Don't do that!" Which brought Uncle Jack right back down.

This time, he wasn't as cordial. He was tired. The wrinkle lines around his eyes were more evident than usual. He was working hard these days. His consulting firm had become so busy, he and the Miller twins' dad had to hire on several more employees for the Dressel Hills-based company, as well as the Denver branch. With a new baby on the way, Uncle Jack was even more stressed, especially because Mom had experienced some problems early in her pregnancy.

"Do we really have to be yelling tonight?" he asked.

"I'm sorry," I said quickly, making no excuses as I wiped Carrie's tongue print off my palm.

"And the rest of you?" He looked at Carrie now, and Phil and Mark.

"I was quiet," Stephie piped up.

He nodded. "Let's try and keep it to a dull roar, okay?"

"This is the last time you'll have to tell us, Daddy," Stephie volunteered. "We promise."

Uncle Jack laughed softly, rumpling her chestnut hair. "It better be."

I decided to remove myself from the room. Being the oldest sibling in the lower level of the house was dangerous. Besides, homework was a good excuse to leave.

Phil and Mark had located a wholesome TV comedy now, and Carrie was inching her way over to investigate it.

Stephie, however, carried Goofey, our cat, upstairs behind me. She followed me all the way to my room. "Here's your Goofey-boy," she said, putting him down gently.

"Thanks." I hoped she wouldn't want to hang around and talk.

But she did. She closed my door behind her and plopped herself down on my window seat. "I wish you'd come home and baby-sit us every day after school," she began.

"Really?"

"Uh-huh." She played with Goofey's tail.

"How come?"

"Because Stan's way too bossy."

I smiled. Nothing new.

"Well, we're all going to have to work together from now on—and especially once our new baby sister comes."

Stephie rolled her eyes. "It's gonna be tough."

"I know." I went over and sat beside her. "You won't be the baby of the family anymore. Right?"

"I'm being bumped."

"You sure are, but won't it be fun to have a real live baby doll around?" I was groping for the right words. What did I know about this? Shoot, I had been four when my little sister came along—not eight, like Stephie. By the time a kid reached this age, she had every right to think it fairly safe to assume that her spot on the birth-order ladder was fixed.

"Do you think Mommy will let me hold her baby?" she asked, her round face full of anticipation.

"I'm sure Mommy will show you how. But you might have to sit down the first couple of times . . . you know, to get the feel of a squirmy bundle."

She giggled about it, and when she was satisfied that Goofey was snuggled down for the night, she left the room.

I set to work reading my chapter for government, hoping I'd remember all the facts when it came time to write the long unit answers. It was a struggle, but not as hard as algebra had been last semester.

Later, I went downstairs for a bowl of strawberry ice cream—my reward for finishing homework in less than two hours.

Stan, however, was snootier than ever. He dished up his ice cream and made a big deal about taking it into the dining room, probably hoping to make me think he was abandoning me on purpose.

I, on the other hand, received his abandonment with sheer delight. *Fine*, I thought as I sat at the kitchen bar, alone. *Act like the jerk that you are.*

And he did. Right up to the moment I said good night. "Mom wants both of us to come straight home tomorrow after school," he stated snidely.

"Whatever." The word slipped out a bit sarcastically, but I didn't care. Stan had wormed his way out of parental discipline once again.

How he managed to pull this one off, I'll never know!

FOUR

Friday, when Jared asked me to sit with him on the bus ride to Denver, I agreed.

Andie, the Miller twins, and Amy-Liz took my decision in stride and sat across from us. Anyone could see that Jared was not the flirt he once was. Actually, the guy was metamorphosing, like most of the other freshmen in our class.

I found it easy to talk to him, the way it had always been with Sean in California. And we had a lot in common, too. Both of us were still waiting to hear back about the manuscripts we'd sent to a small publisher—Jared's entrepreneur uncle, who was eager to work with young authors. Young authors like us.

"Heard anything yet?" I asked, feeling completely comfortable about sitting beside Jared Wilkins now.

He ran his hand through a shock of thick brown hair. "I've heard that they've narrowed down the manuscripts to be considered to seven or eight."

"Really?" This was amazing. "Betcha don't know which ones made the cut."

"My uncle won't tell me anything. I guess it wouldn't be fair, you know, since I'm related ... and since you're my friend." Jared smiled his glorious grin, making his blue eyes dance. "You *are* my friend, aren't you?"

I glanced over at Andie and Paula. They were playing a card game, wrapped up in their own little world. Good! I wasn't wild about someone listening in right about now. Not with Jared starting to talk personal stuff.

Nodding, I said that I was his friend. "And you know what?"

He turned toward me, and for a moment, I thought the old, flirtatious Jared might return. But I was wrong. After all, I'd opened the door wide for whatever smooth-talking reply he might've wanted to offer.

I took a deep breath. "It's a fabulous feeling ... you and me, uh, the way we are now."

He chuckled softly. "I couldn't have said it better myself." And that was that.

We talked about story lines for our own individual projects, and by the time we arrived in Denver, Jared and I were actually discussing the possibility of collaborating on a bigger project. Someday.

Andie couldn't believe it when I told her about it

in the ladies' room, hours later. "This is so-o cool! You're actually getting along with Jared without the mushy stuff."

"I wondered what you'd think," I replied, grinning. Andie had this thing about me linking up with Dressel Hills boys for my friends. She still wasn't all that crazy about Sean's and my long-distance relationship.

Paula and Kayla listened without saying a word, and I wondered if they weren't still a bit leery about Jared. After all, in the past he'd done a fabulous job of fooling every single one of us into thinking he was absolutely crazy over us.

But things were different now—for me, at least. I didn't feel vulnerable anymore. Mostly because of Sean. And Jared knew it, which made all the difference in the world.

I primped and fussed over my hair, which was growing out from its first and only real cutting— back in September, the day before school started. And the perm was perfect now, too—relaxed but not limp. I only wished my spiral-wrapped perm might've behaved this way right from the beginning. But that was another story.

"C'mon, Holly-Heart," Andie said, gathering up my brush and pick and stuffing them into my purse. "This is a choir audition, not a fashion show."

"I know, I know."

"So forget the hair." She pulled me away from the mirror.

I studied her short, bouncy curls. Maybe someday

I'd get brave and have my long hair really whacked off. With that thought, I followed Andie and the other girls out the door and down the hall to the practice room.

Everyone seemed jittery. Not Mrs. Duncan, however. She was confident, poised—ready to go. "Let's knock the judges' socks off," she said, sporting a winning smile.

That got us revved up a bit, and then when we went through our vocalization warm-ups, I could feel the enthusiasm in the air as we worked to make our unison sound strong and clear, like one voice. The spirit of camaraderie and of oneness was powerful. Like an electrical current.

Was it even remotely possible for us to place at this level?

We were certainly dressed for the occasion, wearing our Sunday best. And for a change, Danny Myers fit right in. He was always dressing up for school and other noneventful things, but that was Danny. And thinking about metamorphosing, I had a sneaking suspicion that he was changing too.

❤   ❤   ❤

The auditorium where we were scheduled to sing was bright with overhead lighting and a wall of windows on one side. The judges—two women and two men—sat about a third of the way back, their postures severe and precise, an indication of how scrutinizing they would probably be. Only one of them, the woman on the far left, even so much as cracked a smile.

We filed onto the stage from behind the curtains, taking the risers without a single one of us tripping or falling. When we were all standing with attention-perfect postures, Mrs. Duncan lifted her arms, offering an encouraging smile, then gave us a one-measure cue, and we began. Even as we sang, I sensed that things were going well.

The judges never took their eyes off us. Not once. And when they did look down to write and calculate our points, we had already finished singing our first madrigal.

By the time we'd performed the required audition pieces, I felt emotionally exhausted. All of us had expended so much energy putting out a great sound that we were more than ready to chow down.

Back on the bus, Mrs. Duncan announced that we were going to stop off for supper. Everyone cheered.

Somehow or other, Danny ended up sitting across from me at the restaurant. There had been a time, not so long ago, when he'd had the audacity to admonish me about my eating habits. He'd amazed me by quoting several Proverbs, humiliating me in front of my church friends—all because I'd ordered a giant helping of french fries after having devoured a strawberry sundae with three scoops of ice cream.

Today, however, he said nothing when I smothered my order of fries with ketchup and salt and prepared to eat the Whoppin' Burger complete with pickles, tomatoes, and extra cheese.

What made the difference? I figured it was the

maturation process. The tongue-lashing over my cravings for ice cream and fries had come in the autumn of eighth grade. Danny, now a sophomore, was coming of age. At last!

"So ... how do you think we did today?" I said between bites.

Danny leaned back and sighed. "Well, to tell you the truth, I doubt that we've ever sounded better."

"Really?" Andie chimed in. "That good?"

"Well, it's not quite the same as our youth choir at church," he said. And I knew what he meant. The spiritual unity was missing. Still, lots of us were Christians in the choir, which counted for something. And on top of that, we'd worked hard polishing our repertoire the past few months in preparation for the audition.

Mrs. Duncan came around to chat at each table. Danny asked her opinion on how the choir sounded. Her face lit up. "I can't ever remember a group's sounding so terrific. Honestly, this year's show choir is really tops."

"Do you think we have a shot at the international competitions in Vienna?" I asked.

"It's hard to say. I'm very sure the competition will become more intense as we move up the ladder, but if you kids keep singing as well as you did today—the sky's the limit!"

I had a feeling we all believed her, because when the final tally was announced the following Monday, none of us were too surprised to hear that Dressel Hills Show Choir had taken first place once again!

♥   ♥   ♥

"We're going to Kansas," I told Mom after school on Monday.

"When?" Her arms were wrapped around her protruding stomach as she sat in a sunny spot on her side of the bed.

"Next Saturday and Sunday."

"Well, I hope you won't be gone when the baby decides to make her appearance." She looked a tad bit worried.

"Do you think there's a possibility of that?"

"Holly-Heart, I don't want to spoil your opportunity to sing with the choir," she said, encouraging me to come around and sit near her. "But I'll be needing your help here with the other children when I go to the hospital."

"What about Uncle Jack, can't he help?"

She smiled. "Your stepdad wants to be present for the birth of our baby."

I wondered about that. Hadn't he witnessed a live, natural birth? After all, he was the father of four other children.

But the more I thought about it, the more I suspected that his deceased wife, my aunt Marla, may not have been the type to want her husband in the birthing room, coaching the delivery.

"What about Stan? Can't he help out if you go into labor while I'm gone?"

Her forehead shifted up, creating lines. Lines that probably meant she didn't think my brousin could handle it, or worse, she didn't think he

31

would cooperate enough to pull it off. More than likely, the latter was true.

"Stan's not as eager to assist with the younger children, if you know what I mean," she was saying.

"Right," I fired back. "Isn't it just a little too obvious?"

"Now, don't go jumping to conclusions. Stan has his reasons." She paused, then continued. "Your brother's making his way through some very advanced high school classes these days."

Sounded to me like she was sticking up for him. "C'mon, Mom, don't you see? He's gonna use any excuse he can."

She was silent for a moment, looking tired and radiant both. Her golden-blonde hair hung in soft waves around her face, creating almost an ethereal impression.

But I wasn't dense. I could see she didn't need her oldest daughter giving her grief about household chores and the possibility of having to babysit during her labor.

My mother was pushing forty and not as spry as she had been years before, when she carried Carrie and me to full term. Besides, she'd suffered a miscarriage back when I was in grade school. I wanted to go gentle on her. "It's just that Stan expects me to pick up the pieces for him all the time, you know, sort of be his backup."

Mom nodded. "I understand how you must feel."

"I really don't enjoy being Plan B," I said, but in this case, I didn't relish the idea of being Plan A, either. Especially if it meant jeopardizing my plans for choir.

"Is there a good chance the baby will come early?" I said softly, afraid the very question might stir her up, get her thinking about it.

She touched my hand and held it. "I don't think we have anything to worry about, Holly-Heart. Many prayers have been going up for our baby, so you must relax about this, too."

I gave Mom a kiss on her cheek. Everything was under control in the baby department. Mom would be just fine.

What a relief. I was going to Kansas next weekend!

FIVE

There were no signs of false labor, premature labor, or any other kind, as Mom waved to me from the living-room window early the following Saturday morning.

Uncle Jack backed the family van out of the driveway, and we headed to the school parking lot, near downtown. The city school district had come up with the revenue for a chartered bus, maybe because Dressel Hills High had never placed in anything cultural. Oh, sure, there were always trophies for football and track, but never the arts.

I had a fabulous feeling about all this. Our show choir was about to put Dressel Hills, Colorado, on the map!

While it was still dark, we boarded the bus. I waved good-bye to Uncle Jack, who stood tall and proud along with the other parents. I was surprised there was no media coverage of the event. It was definitely a first.

By three o'clock in the afternoon, Central Standard Time, we had arrived in Topeka, Kansas, warmed up and ready to outperform ourselves. The trip had taken less than nine hours, with no stops for lunch—we'd brought snacks and sack lunches with us. And the bus had rest-room facilities.

Most of us had snoozed off and on, so no one was really too wiped out from the trip. Except maybe the driver. Anyway, we did our best when it came time to hit the practice room. Mrs. Duncan, grinning hard, gave us a pep talk before our audition.

"We're this far, aren't we? Is this great or what?" Her hazel-brown eyes twinkled as she looked out at all of us perched on the risers. "Anybody here not ready to show the world who's the best high school choir around?"

I smiled at her comment and stood up with the others when she gave the familiar motion. We worked through several interpretative spots on "Hallelujah" by American composer Randall Thompson. Man, did I love this piece—and sang my heart out. Paula and Kayla did too. In fact, as I glanced around, everyone seemed jazzed up about where we were and what we were about to do.

After the audition, we found the nearest fast-food place and pigged out. Once again, Danny Myers ended up sitting at the same table with me. He seemed more mellow than I'd ever remembered him. And as he talked, I noticed the preachy edge was missing from his voice.

"What's with Danny?" I asked Andie later that night. We were staying at one of the big hotels near Interstate 70—four girls to a room. Paula and Kayla were my two other roommates.

"Danny?" Andie stared at me. "Are you trying to tell us something?" She glanced at the Miller twins, who, by now, were listening intently.

"Yeah, Danny. He's different . . . I think," I said.

"Well, you must wanna be a preacher's wife," Andie said. "Which really is fine with me. At least you won't be going off to California to get married."

"Oh, Andie, please! Who said anything about getting married." I opened my suitcase and pulled out my pajamas.

"Danny's definitely waiting for the right girl to come along," Kayla spoke up. "He says he's not going to date, but he's going to wait for God to bring the right mate to him."

I thought about that. "Hey, I like that."

Paula dug around in her suitcase and pulled out a slim paperback. She waved it in my face. "Here, take a look at this. I think, very possibly, this is where Danny first heard about his approach to finding a wife."

"Really?" I turned the book over and read the back. "This sounds really interesting."

Andie came over and peered at the book. "Maybe you've just found some food for thought."

I looked at her. "Huh?"

"You know, the next time Danny shows up at your table, you two could discuss this—kind of common ground for conversation."

"Now you're teasing me." I handed the book to Paula.

"No, really. I mean it, Holly. The guy's really tuned into what he believes is the best way to discover God's plan for a life-mate—simply wait." Andie wasn't joking at all. "It sounds unbelievable, I know, but I guess we'll just have to read it for ourselves."

"Where'd Danny get the book?" I asked.

"The church library has it," she said. "Just came in."

"So ... how soon will you be finished reading it?" I asked Paula.

"I'm on the next-to-last chapter." She pulled on her terry-cloth robe. "But there's a long waiting list at church, I understand." She showed me where she was in the book, then while Kayla, Andie, and I engaged in girl talk, Paula went to read in the corner of the hotel room, nearest the table lamp.

I couldn't help glancing over at her every few minutes. The book intrigued me. I couldn't wait to read it too.

❤   ❤   ❤

The next day, we were approaching the outskirts of Junction City on our way back to Colorado when Paula handed the book to me. I was so eager to start it that when Jared came and asked me if I wanted to talk, I declined. Politely, of course.

"Do you mind?" I said, apologetically.

He spied the book in my hands and shrugged. "Well, if that's what you're reading, fine."

"You've read it?"

He grinned. "It's really ... uh, different, but great." And before he left to go back to his seat, he said, "When you finish it, let's talk, okay?"

"Sure." But I didn't realize how riveting a nonfiction book could be. I didn't want to put it down! The concepts made perfect, good sense. And they were based on biblical principles—romance, God's way.

Andie tried to get my attention several times. When I looked up, she was frowning. "Didn't you hear the announcement?"

"What announcement?" I looked around. Choir members were raising their hands for something.

"They're doing a head count for the McDonald's in Salina. Do you want a burger or something else?"

"What are the choices?" I asked.

She told me. It was either burgers with the works—no special orders since we were only going to stop for a few minutes—or fish sandwiches.

"Better tell Mrs. Duncan you were spacing out," Andie admonished.

I trudged up to the front of the bus and gave my burger order. When I returned, the book on God's will for a mate was nowhere to be seen.

"Andie!"

"What?"

"Where's the book?"

"What book?"

"C'mon, you know." I could see she'd set me up.

"Oh, this?" She held it up, wearing a smirk.

"It would be nice if I could actually finish it before you start it."

She was reluctant—already had her finger stuck in the second page. "Well, I absolutely have to read the rest . . . and soon."

"Okay, I'll hurry." The truth was I didn't want to hurry through it. This kind of courtship book didn't come along very often, and everyone was falling all over themselves to read it. At least, people who were close to marrying age. Not that I thought I was, it was just that sometimes I found myself thinking about what my future would be like. Who I would marry or if I would at all . . .

My mom's marriage record wasn't exactly the best, that was obvious. She and Daddy had suffered through a separation and then divorce by the time I was eight years old. I was hardly old enough to know what was going on, but old enough to know it hurt. Bad. Their divorce had left a skeptical imprint stamped in my mind, especially about the happily-ever-after kind of love.

Now, though, Mom seemed settled and happy with Jack Patterson, and they were starting a brand-new family together. The big difference, the way I saw it, was that Mom and Uncle Jack were both dedicated Christians. And they worked hard at their relationship, which was something lots of couples with kids seemed to neglect.

Anyway, I wanted my marriage to last forever. And I knew if I could just follow the radical precepts in Paula's book, it might happen for me.

Someday.

Thinking about what I'd read—about giving myself totally to Jesus, in short, falling in love with *him*—made me wonder if the unique message of the book had been the reason for the change in Jared. Danny, too.

Quickly, I found my place and began reading again, blocking out Andie's chatter with Paula and Kayla. Even a stopover for fast food couldn't keep my nose out of the book.

If only I had read something like this earlier. I could have saved myself the heartache of the boy/girl thing and of "giving away" my intimate emotions to a guy.

I could hardly wait to write Sean about my fabulous new discovery.

SIX

In Hays, Kansas, I turned the book over to Andie just as I spotted the city limits sign. She was thrilled and dived right into it.

On the opposite side of the bus, Paula, Kayla, and I discussed some of the alternatives to modern dating as presented in the book. Things like hanging out in groups and being platonic friends with the opposite sex. And parental involvement in a choice of a mate. Most of all, being patient as God worked out his loving plan for our lives.

"I'd give anything if I could've skipped over those all-consuming crushes of my life," I admitted softly, glancing around to make sure neither Danny nor Jared were in earshot.

"I know what you mean," Paula said. "The dating game is for the birds. You get hurt because the boy might end up liking someone else after a while."

Kayla nodded her head. "That's so very true."

Paula continued, "Some people say you can't find God's choice unless you date lots of people. But waiting for God's perfect timing—waiting for *him* to bring along your life-mate—makes a lot more sense."

"Spiritual sense, too," I whispered.

Andie perked up her ears. "Hey, what am I missing over there?"

"Nothing compared to that," I replied, pointing to the book.

"Oh, good." And she went back to reading.

❤   ❤   ❤

I did finally have a chance to talk with Jared before our bus made its way over the first mountain pass west of Denver, Colorado.

"I don't know if I ever apologized for hurting you the way I did last year," Jared said at one of the stops to stretch our legs.

"Well, you did," I reminded him. "Many times."

He smiled, but not that dreamy, flirty smile of his. "I wish I'd known then what I know now about trusting the Lord for my romantic future."

"You're not the only one." We walked back toward the bus, and I felt joyful. Jared and I really were good friends now. The old boy/girl thing was gone between us. Both of us wanted God's best for the other—the way it always should've been.

Andie was saying some of the same things when

she finished reading, later. In fact, it seemed that half the bus was buzzing about the book.

"Doesn't it beat a Marty Leigh mystery?" Paula asked.

"All to pieces," I said, realizing that I might consider reading nonfiction for a change.

Andie chuckled. "I wondered when the three of you would come to your senses about mysteries."

"They're better than those silly romance novels you read," I countered.

Andie shook her head. "You mean the romance novels I used to read. Now"—and here she glanced at the book in her lap—"now I'm not so sure."

"Maybe someday I'll sprinkle in some of these ideas into one of my novels for teen girls." Sounded like the perfect plan to me.

"Don't forget, I get the first dedication," Paula said with a smile, showing off her perfect, white teeth.

"Why, because she showed you the book?" Andie retorted. "But I'm your best friend, don't forget."

"We're all best friends," I said. And I could tell by the twinkle in her eye, Andie understood.

❤   ❤   ❤

It was almost dusk when the bus pulled into the parking lot of the high school. Mrs. Duncan told us to go home and go to bed. "You're all excused from turning in homework assignments tomorrow. But don't take advantage of your other teachers," she advised.

Billy Hill raised his hand. "When will we know if we placed?"

"No later than next Thursday."

The kids groaned, including me. Could we wait that long?

I hugged my girlfriends good-bye, promising to meet them for lunch in the school cafeteria tomorrow, Monday.

It didn't take long for me to spot our family van, but when I looked more closely, I noticed Stan sitting in the driver's seat.

I shoved away the thought of complaining. At least I had a ride home.

As it turned out, Stan had taken time out from the Sunday evening service to come for me. No heading home or resting for me. He drove back to church, where Mom, Uncle Jack, and all the kids were sitting in the seventh pew from the front. On the left side, as usual.

We tiptoed in and sat in the back—Stan and I. Exhausted from my whirlwind weekend, I let myself slouch down in the seat a bit. Stan shot me a superior, almost parental look.

"I'm beat," I whispered.

He looked away, acting disgusted. And that's how things got started again between us.

All through the following week, Stan was his non-adorable self, chewing me out whenever possible. Over the weirdest stuff, too.

For instance, Tuesday he came into my room, where I was folding some baby blankets in the crib.

He scowled as he watched, then started to remind me that he was not, under any circumstances, going to feed, change, or burp Mom's new baby.

"Hey, don't tell me about it," I said.

His face flushed red. "Holly, you're taking things for granted about this baby—"

"Who isn't even born yet," I interrupted, studying him. "I can only hope that April doesn't turn out to have any of your sinister qualities."

He shook his head. "You're grasping at straws, girl."

"Here, catch." I threw a pink plastic baby bottle at him. "It's high time you get the feel of things. Someday you'll wish you knew how to do all this wonderful baby stuff—for your own son or daughter. Or, hey, here's a thought: maybe, just maybe, you'll want to help your wife out, what about that?"

He snorted something, which I didn't quite catch. And really didn't want to.

"You know, there's really nothing sissy at all about any of this," I offered.

He scratched his head, like he was trying to figure me out. "I told you, Holly. It's a girl thing." And with that, he threw the bottle back to me and left the room.

Frustrated, I went to my door and closed it. Ah, peace, at last. And time for another journal entry. Maybe, I thought, if I write down my frustrations, I'll feel better.

Tuesday, April 9th

The oldest brousin is hopeless, as in completely gone. I'm referring to Stan, which should come as no surprise.

When I look back over the pages of this secret diary, it's obvious that the boy has dished out nothing but harassment ever since his father married my mother.

Now . . . on a lighter side. Mrs. Duncan told us today that she'll have the outcome of our auditions in two more days. Andie suspects that she already knows, but is waiting till our principal returns from an administrative conference before announcing the news.

Anyway, between Mom's bouts with sleepless nights (she really does think the baby might come early!), and the possibility of show choir going to Washington during spring break, I'm freaked out.

If only Stan would cool it with his ridiculous macho remarks!

SEVEN

Thursday, April 11th

Things couldn't be better! We're flying to the nation's capital in exactly eight days—the high school show choir, that is.

Our choral status has finally hit the papers, and there was an exclusive interview with Mrs. Duncan on the evening news.

My friends can hardly believe we're going, especially Paula and Kayla, who have relatives in Pennsylvania. Paula's going to ask Mrs. Duncan tomorrow about getting them in to see the auditions.

My family? Now that's a problem. Mom's so sure that the baby is coming early. And Uncle Jack wants to talk to me tonight after supper. Shoot, I can almost imagine what he's going to say. I can only hope the baby arrives before I leave!

To round off the fabulous things in my life, a letter from Sean arrived today. He's planning to attend college days at George Washington University, which isn't far from the location of our audition. (I looked it up on the Internet.) Of course, he has no idea I'm going back there that same weekend, but I'm sure he'll want to know. So . . . one letter-writing session coming up!

After supper dishes were cleared off the table and loaded in the dishwasher, Uncle Jack sat me down in the living room. Mom had already gone upstairs to get off her feet, which seemed to be swelling, my stepdad informed me.

Stan was out with some friends, and the rest of my siblings were either tending to homework or waiting for family devotions to begin.

"I think we need to talk," Uncle Jack began softly. His wavy, brown hair looked disheveled from the long day, and a five o'clock shadow stubbled his chin. "Your mother and I are thrilled for you about the high school choir competitions back east. There's only one little hitch."

Here it comes, I thought.

"If the baby comes early, we're going to need you here, Holly."

Mom had already said the same thing, in so many words. But hearing it from Uncle Jack made it sound terribly final.

"But we're supposed to fly out a week from tomorrow," I told him.

The school board had decided to pitch in half of each plane ticket. The rest had come from Parent

Teachers' Association fund-raisers—in case we got to go.

Uncle Jack glanced at the calendar on the lamp table near the couch. "Let's see, that's Friday, April 19?"

I nodded. The baby was due exactly six days later, on April 25.

Uncle Jack scrunched his lips. "That's cutting it close."

"I'm really praying about this," I volunteered, "so if it's okay with you, let's not plan for the worst."

He chuckled good-naturedly, and I felt the heaviness lift.

Soon, he was calling for the rest of the family, and instead of having devotions in the living room, we gathered in the master bedroom upstairs. That way, Mom's swollen feet and ankles could be elevated, and she could relax.

I listened to the Scripture reading, but couldn't keep my mind on the story that followed. I was too deep in thought, pondering how incredible it was going to be to sing and compete against America's best ensemble groups.

Remembering Miss Hess, my choral director from junior high, I wondered how she must be feeling about the news. Surely, it was a direct result of her careful training that had brought the choir to this present level. I decided to stop by the junior high after school tomorrow and pay her a visit.

After prayers were said, and Mom let Carrie and

Stephie "talk" to their baby sister in her stomach, I hurried off to my room to write to Sean.

Andie called in the middle of my letter. Evidently, Stan had come home, picking up the phone on the first ring. He shouted up the stairs to me, his voice sounding polite in spite of the volume, probably because Uncle Jack was sitting nearby.

I took the hall phone. "Hey, what's up?"

"Hi." Andie paused. "What's Stan doing home?"

"He lives here." I giggled.

"I know that, silly. But I thought you said he was going out with some friends."

"They must be done doing whatever it was they did."

We both burst into laughter.

"Seriously," she said, "I was wondering if Stan's read that book on praying for God's choice in a mate."

"Oh . . . I get it."

"No, it's not what you're thinking," she insisted.

"You mean you don't still like my stepbrother?"

"C'mon, Holly. You should know what I mean. After reading that book and all."

"Where's the book now?"

"Paula returned it to the church resource center. It probably got snatched up by the next person on the list."

"Which was?"

"Wish I knew," she said.

"Well, if you're so desperate for it, why don't you

buy it?" I suggested. "The Christian bookstore should have it."

"Great idea. I'll check it out tomorrow after school."

"Okay, but I was hoping you'd come along with me to say 'hi' to Miss Hess."

"Hey, that would be fun. Should I see if Paula and Kayla wanna come, too?"

"Perfect." So it was set, we were going to stop by and visit our old stomping grounds. And a favorite teacher.

However, not once during the course of our phone chatting did I bring up my conversation with Uncle Jack. No sense having Andie worry about something that most likely wouldn't happen anyway.

EIGHT

The following Monday, Sean Hamilton called long-distance. "We could meet somewhere in D.C. and have lunch." He sounded very excited.

"How long will you be there?" I asked.

"Just three days ... my plane leaves early Tuesday morning. You?"

"We're leaving this Friday and coming back next Wednesday."

"Great! We should be able to squeeze in some time on Monday to tour the monuments or see the Smithsonian. Okay with you?"

"Well, I think our director is scheduling a tour for the choir on Monday," I replied. "Maybe it would work out for you to join us."

Sean didn't hesitate. "That'd be fine." He went on to give me a contact number where he could be reached, and I did the same. "This'll be really terrific, Holly," he said. "I'm looking forward to seeing you again."

I could almost see Sean's face. His voice sounded like he was really happy. So was I!

❤   ❤   ❤

The visit back to the junior high building the next day brought with it nostalgic feelings. Andie got it started. She talked about the day the ambulance came and took Jared Wilkins away, after a mishap on the ropes during timed tests in P.E. Then, one after another, Paula, Kayla, and I began to recount the events of our two years in those halls of ivy.

"Does everyone remember when Danny Myers had a big crush on Holly?" Andie asked, looking at Paula and Kayla.

"I think he still does," Paula said. She fluffed her hair and grinned at me.

"Crushes come and crushes go," I said, thinking about the cool book with the awesome information about waiting for God's will. "But true love, now that's what I'm anxious for!"

"Remember, the most important thing is to remain simply good friends until God brings along the right person." Kayla was sounding like a quote from the book.

"But how will we know when our future husband shows up?" Andie asked, glancing at me.

"The book says to be in prayer about it, asking God to show you—to make it very clear—and the timing will be perfect, too."

"Man, it's hard to picture it happening like that when we've been programmed so differently," Kayla commented. "I mean, the media plays up romance and sex as though it were the thing to do. But I know not everyone conducts their life that way."

Andie agreed. "It's like Hollywood and the TV networks are trying to brainwash us to believe a lie."

By the time we arrived upstairs in Miss Hess's cozy choir room, we were completely sold on the book's approach to romance—God's way.

"Well, hello there, girls," Miss Hess said, looking up from her desk. "What brings you here?"

"Haven't you heard about us?" Andie asked, her dark eyes shining.

"I certainly have," our former choir director replied. "I've been following the audition results very closely. You know, Mrs. Duncan and I are good friends."

"Cool," I said. "Do you and Mrs. Duncan confer with each other about music?"

She got up and went to the piano, leaning on the back of it the way she always used to. "You may not know this, but Mrs. Duncan and I worked out some of the scores for *The Sound of Music* together last year."

"You did?" I don't know why I found this so interesting. Maybe because there was a comfortable link back to seventh- and eighth-grade days. "Are you doing another musical this year?"

"I guess you could call it that. We're doing a Victorian melodrama complete with heroine, hero, and a wicked villain. It's written by our own school librarian, and right now, I'm putting the finishing touches on the olio, which is a collection of musical performances, following the actual drama."

"Wow, can we see what you're doing?" I inched toward the desk. It was the same desk I'd snooped at last year, when I was too impatient to wait for the posted list of student characters in *The Sound of Music*.

Miss Hess, her clothes as stylish and colorful as ever, agreed to show us her work. "We really have quite a strong orchestra this year," she pointed out, showing the various orchestral scores she'd hand-written.

"Whoa, this looks tedious," Andie commented.

"Yeah," I agreed. "And when's the show?"

"May 10 and 11 ... we're doing it two consecutive nights."

"Just like last year," I said as fond memories came flying back.

"Ah, the good old days," Andie teased, putting her arm around me. "I think Holly misses the spotlight."

We laughed and talked for a while longer. Then I got brave and asked Miss Hess if she knew anything about Mr. Barnett, her student teacher from last year.

"Oh, yes, I certainly do." She said it as though he were a special friend. "Mr. Barnett is a high school drama coach in St. Paul, Minnesota."

"Really?" Just hearing her mention his name brought all the crazy, crushy days zooming back.

"He and I correspond occasionally," she volunteered. "I think we were very fortunate to have Mr. Barnett come here."

I didn't say another word. Not with Andie and Paula staring at me like I might still have feelings for the guy. Of course, I didn't. All that was far behind me now.

"Are each of you in show choir?" asked Miss Hess.

"We sure are," Andie said. "And we're loving every minute of it."

"And you're the accompanist," she said, grinning at Andie.

That's when I spoke up. "She's fabulous. You should hear her play the interlude to some of our songs." Which got Andie an invitation to show off.

She sat right down, without being begged, and played.

"Oh, I miss having you around," Miss Hess said. "Good pianists are a dime a dozen, but pianists who can follow a director, now there's a dying breed."

Andie beamed, and I was proud of my friend.

We said our good-byes, all of us leaving the building with a sad, lumpy feeling in our throats. That's probably why no one said anything until we got out to the sidewalk.

"Man, I miss that place," Andie said.

"Me too." I linked arms with my girlfriends.

Paula and Kayla smiled sentimental, look-alike smiles as we waited for the city bus. The bus stop was across the street and down about a half block, facing the Soda Straw, one of our favorite spots, even now that we were hotshot freshmen.

"Do you remember when Holly dressed up like a Catholic nun and eavesdropped on Mr. Barnett and Miss Hess at the Soda Straw?" Andie said.

I groaned. "Oh, not that."

"Hilarious," Paula said. The twins laughed and teased me even more.

"Well, if that's the case," I piped up, "what about the promise I made to your mom, Andie—at the Soda Straw?"

"You promised to watch over me when I went to California with you last summer," she said. "What a mess I got myself into."

"No kidding," I said.

The bus was coming, and it was probably a good thing. Sometimes rehashing the past can dig up pain you'd rather not deal with in front of your best friends.

I dropped the subject, and we turned our attention toward the choir trip and our hopes for a win at nationals.

"Even if we don't place, it's going to be a wonderful experience for everyone," Paula offered.

"My mom keeps saying the same thing," said Andie.

I kept quiet, letting the others voice their feelings. It wasn't time to tell anyone about Sean's and my plans to meet. They might think I wasn't sincere when I agreed with them that romance God's way was the best way.

NINE

My mother started having labor pains early Wednesday morning, two days before the scheduled choir trip. And eight days before she was supposed to be due!

I didn't even want to go to school, I was that upset. Here she was going to have the baby early and spoil my hopes for singing at the audition. And for seeing Sean again.

Of course, it was all very selfish the way I felt. But the frantic, hopeless feeling persisted and, by noon, I'd called the hospital twice.

Andie hovered close to the pay phone as I listened to the nurse on the other end. "Did your mom have her baby yet?" she whispered.

I shook my head and hung up, then scuffed my foot against the waxed floor. "Mom's definitely in labor, but not even close to delivering. I don't believe this!" I moaned and stomped off to the cafeteria, Andie trailing behind.

"Are you really sure your stepdad meant you'd have to stay home from choir auditions?" she asked.

"Uncle Jack never talks in riddles. It was clear, all right. He wants to be in the delivery room when his baby is born, which means I'm needed at home."

"Oh, Holly," she wailed, "I thought you were praying about this!"

"I have been." I turned to look at her. "Have you?"

"Not actually prayed . . . no."

"Well, if you're so worried, why not?" It was a harsh thing to say, and I was immediately sorry.

"Look, the way I see it, something big has to happen in order for you to go to Washington, D.C.," she insisted.

"Such as?"

"Like maybe . . ." She thought for a moment. "Like if your mom has the baby today or even tonight, she might be home by Friday."

"Nice try." It wasn't really, but Andie seemed desperate to help. "There's another reason why Mom's gotta have this baby soon . . . like today," I said as we waited in the hot lunch line.

Andie frowned, and I knew she had no clue. "Why?"

"Because of Sean Hamilton."

"Sean? I don't get it."

"Well, it just so happens that he's going to be

visiting the campus at George Washington University during 'College Days'—checking out the premed program this very weekend." I didn't say that he and I were hoping to spend some time together. One thing at a time.

"Oh, so now you tell me." She reached for a fruit salad on a bed of semi-wilted lettuce.

"You're gonna eat that?" I joked.

"Oh, no, you don't. You don't get off that easy!"

We paid for our lunches and headed over to the area where we usually sat—as far away from the seniors as possible, that is. But close enough to the big window to enjoy the sunny, springlike day.

Andie stared me down until I started explaining things. Like how I was excited to know that Sean would be in Washington, D.C., and how I'd already talked to Mrs. Duncan about him coming along on one of our tours.

"Really?" She stopped eating, her fork dangling between her fingers. "Then you must've been fooling me about waiting for the perfect mate."

I figured she might think this. "Don't you understand? Sean and I have been friends—just friends—from the very beginning. He and I are not romantically involved. Nothing like that."

"Yeah, right. When have I heard that before?"

"Well, it's true."

"Then why do you want to see him so badly?"

"Both of us want to see each other. What's so terrible about that?"

"Nothing, I just—"

"Look, I don't think we're gonna see eye to eye on this," I interrupted. "Why can't you just believe me? Sean and I really are just good friends. And we're only teenagers, for pete's sake!"

She tilted her head, unconsciously questioning me from across the table. "Would you be willing to forfeit seeing him?"

"Why . . . because of the book?"

"Well, that and because it sounds like your parents are counting on you here at home."

I sighed. "First of all, not seeing Sean has nothing to do with waiting or not waiting for God's will, and second . . . how long does it take to have a baby?"

The answer to that came hours later. Nine hours to be exact.

I was trying to get Carrie and Stephie to stop whining about going to bed, while Mark and Phil insisted that their dad had told them they could stay up till he got home from the hospital.

"But he might not be home till midnight or later," I explained.

"So?" Mark said.

I talked straight to my droopy-eyed brousins. "The way I see it, you two can stay up as late as you like. Just don't complain tomorrow when you have to get up early for school, all tired out."

Man, I was really beginning to sound like somebody's parent!

Stan was no help. He hid away in his room, shutting out the world of his family, while I tried desperately to cope with the real possibility of missing out on a school trip of a lifetime. All the while attempting to keep the house running and my younger siblings on their usual schedules. I was barely holding my own.

♥   ♥   ♥

"Lord, please let Mom have her baby soon," I prayed, getting myself ready for bed. "It's not just because I want to go to Washington on Friday— although that would be fabulous—it's more like: so I won't lose my sanity staying here!"

I pulled on my warmest bathrobe and padded downstairs in my slippers. My siblings were all tucked in for the night. It was time for me to have a little talk with Stan.

There was a light shining from under his door. Good! He was still up.

"It's open," he called, when I knocked.

I poked my head in just a bit. "You busy?"

"Who me?" He laughed, and I hoped this might be easier than I'd first thought.

Honestly, I didn't want to step foot in his room— the epitome of messy. Everywhere I looked, clothes were draped over chairs, strewn around on the floor . . . even dangling off a lamp shade.

"Dad's not gonna be thrilled about this," I said, referring to the major pigsty.

"Dad's not here, is he?" came the reply.

"No, but I am." I held my breath and moved past the doorway and into the room a few inches. "Your room doesn't meet my standards, so would it be possible to meet me in the kitchen, say, in five minutes?"

He glanced at his watch, then up at me, a quizzical look on his face. "Now's fine."

It was the answer I was hoping for. I turned and left the eyesore behind. It seemed weird being the only one up in the house—except for Stan, of course. Knowing that my younger brothers and sisters were snuggled safely into their beds, and most likely asleep by now, created a peculiar response in me. This emotion I didn't fully understand. Maybe it came out of a sense of responsibility (which I wasn't exactly sure I was ready to take on), or just plain being needed. A response Stan sure could use about now!

The phone rang, and I jumped to get it. "Hello?"

"Holly, it's Uncle Jack. I wanted to check in with you before you headed for bed. Is everything going okay?"

Did I dare tell him about my chaotic evening with his children? Should I mention the horrid state of affairs in Stan's room? Or Stan's lousy attitude?

"Holly?" He sounded worried.

"Uh, things are fine. How's Mom?"

"It's become quite a struggle, I'm afraid. The docs are talking surgery—Caesarean section."

"Oh, no."

"Yeah, I know. I'm not wild about it either, but if it's going to mean the difference between—"

"Mom's all right, isn't she?" I blurted.

"She's fine, it's the baby we're worried about," came the tense reply.

I cringed. I really didn't want to hear any more. Right now, the only thing I could think about was Mom. If she lost this baby, too, well ... she just couldn't!

"Please don't worry, honey," Uncle Jack was saying.

Now he tells me, I thought.

"I'll pray," I said.

"That's right ... pray," he whispered, and the thought occurred to me that I'd never heard him so choked up.

We continued talking—about what to do if Stephie became frightened in the night, or if Mark needed his inhaler ... stuff like that. As for me, I didn't mention the choir trip looming before me. Or the fact that his firstborn son was now standing over me, glaring.

"Please tell Mom I love her," I said.

"I sure will, and she loves you, too, Holly. We both do. And thanks for everything you and Stan are doing to help."

Stan? What was he doing?

I hung up after we said good-bye and felt completely at liberty to unload on my brousin. "Your father seems to think that you're involved here, helping keep the home fires burning, but what he doesn't know is you're shirking your duty as a member of this family!"

I brushed past him and went to the other side of

the kitchen, leaning on the sink the way Mom did sometimes when we were having a serious talk.

"What're you so high and mighty about?" he muttered.

"Mom's having trouble," I said. "She might need to have a C-section."

"That bad?"

"The doctors must think so." I paused a moment before going on. "What's really bad around here, though, is you. Don't you realize I'll probably end up having to miss the choir auditions? And it's all because of you!"

"Me?" He was playing dumb, a role he knew well.

"Look, if you were half the man you think you are, you'd get off your duff and actually help out around here."

"Why? So you can go off and see your boyfriend?" he jeered.

"Sean's not my boyfriend anymore than you're a responsible big brother." The words stung the air as they flew off my lips.

Stan pulled out a bar stool and sat down, flashing angry eyes at me.

"Think about it—what is it you do when you're needed the most?" I said, bringing the focus of things back to him. "I'll tell you ... you hide! You run and hide, that's what!"

Stan smirked. "I told you before, I'm not into kids ... or babies, whatever."

Glancing around, I played into his ridiculous

comment, paving the way for my own comeback. "I don't see any babies around. But there sure are a bunch of sleeping kids in this house."

He shook his head arrogantly. "You don't get it, do you? You're the girl, and I'm the guy. Girls are supposed to do this stuff."

"Since when?"

"Since the beginning of time," he said. "Since Adam tilled the soil and Eve raised the kids."

"So ... why aren't you out plowing or planting? What're you waiting for?"

"You're carrying this too far, Holly," he retorted. It was obvious he had no logical, sane response. His deceased mother would be turning over in her grave about now.

"Someday, if God permits, and I almost pray he doesn't, you'll probably marry some nice young woman. The two of you will eventually want to have children, but that's where the picture goes blurry. The nice husband and father ... where is he?"

Suddenly, he got up, almost knocking over the bar stool. His abrupt movement startled me. "Are you finished?" he demanded. "Because if you are, I'm going to bed."

I didn't have the nerve to continue. The message had been brought home loud and clear. I could only hope my ignorant brousin would take it to heart.

My dream, and possibly my future, depended on it.

T E N

The sound of birds awakened me the next morning. Imagine! Birds this early in Colorado high country.

I was so disoriented that I nearly forgot Mom and the baby and my dilemma about choir trip. Glancing at the alarm clock, I discovered that I had a good twenty minutes before the alarm was scheduled to sound off.

Instead of nestling back down under the covers, I got up and tiptoed to the other end of the hall. To Mom and Uncle Jack's bedroom. No one was there, because they'd spent the night in the hospital, it appeared.

I closed the door and hurried to the phone, dialing the hospital—directly to Mom's private room.

Uncle Jack answered on the first ring. He sounded

groggy, and I could almost visualize him having slept in a chair all night. Probably at Mom's bedside.

"I was going to give you a call later, but you beat me to it," he began after we exchanged greetings. "Your mother, stubborn gal she is, was so determined to have this baby naturally. But along about three-thirty this morning, she and the docs decided it was best for the baby to take it by surgery."

"So my sister's already born? She's here ... and okay?"

"She certainly is," he said, pride bursting from every word. "And wait'll you see her. April Michelle is an absolute apple dumplin'—a real charmer."

"And Mom? How's Mom?"

"Kind of out of it," he explained. "She'll probably stay here over the weekend, at least. I won't be surprised if they keep her."

There goes the choir trip, I agonized.

"I really do wish the timing had been different," he said apologetically. "I'm counting on you, Holly-Heart."

"I know," was all I could muster.

"Well, I have a feeling there'll be other choir trips." He was saying it out of sympathy. Nothing else. What he didn't know was—there would never be another moment in time like this for me. Not for the Dressel Hills High School Show Choir. Not ever.

And Sean? I knew I might as well forget about seeing him again for a very long time.

"Holly? You still there?"

"Oh ... uh-huh." I felt torn between the missed trip and the announcement of my new baby sister. "How much does April weigh?" I asked.

"Eight pounds and eleven ounces ... she's filled out beautifully ... and pink! I don't know when I've seen a prettier newborn baby."

"I can't wait to see her."

"Stan'll have to bring all of you up to the hospital after school."

With the mention of "school," my alarm clock went off in my room. I could hear its muffled, yet shrill tones coming through the door.

"I think I'd better spread the news here," I said. "Besides, I've never had to get this many kids off to school by myself."

"What do you mean?" He sounded irked. "Isn't Stan pulling his share of the load?"

Do I dare tell on him? I sighed, trying to decide what to do.

"Holly? What's going on?"

Desperate for some adult intervention, I struggled. "I guess ... I think things'll be okay."

"You think?"

"Oh, it's probably no big deal." I could feel myself caving in. "But Stan and I are sorta on the outs right now. He doesn't see why he should have to help so much—it's women's work."

Uncle Jack chuckled. "Stan said that?"

"In so many words."

"Well, that's going to stop, and I'll be the one to see to it."

I groaned. "Stan'll never let me live this down."

"Don't you worry, kiddo. I'll handle this in such a way as to conceal your side of the story."

We said good-bye, and I made a mad dash for the bathroom. I figured if I showered before Carrie and Stephanie got up, most everything else would go smoothly.

❤   ❤   ❤

I thought wrong.

First of all, nobody wanted to get up. Secondly, I looked everywhere for the plug-in—the electric frying pan didn't work without it—but found nothing. This meant nobody would be having any protein, as in bacon or sausage, with their breakfast. Not today.

"Why don'tcha make waffles, like Mom does?" Carrie hollered from the nearest bar stool.

"Why don't you keep your ideas to yourself?" I snapped. "We don't have time for such niceties."

"Yeah, you didn't get up quick enough," Stephanie said, pouting.

"Neither did you." I motioned for her to wash the toothpaste off her chin. "Today's going to be a cereal and toast day, and if anyone has a problem with it, he or she can just sign up for extra chores."

Mark's eyes bugged out, and he marched out of the kitchen and into the dining room, obviously upset.

Phil adjusted his wire rims and gave me a pensive, academic stare. "Has anyone seen the *Wall Street Journal*?"

"It's probably still out on the driveway," I replied. "If you want it, go get it."

"Eew, she's mad," Stephie whispered to Carrie, showing her dimples.

I turned around, handed her a full carton of milk, and smiled as sweetly as I possibly could under the circumstances. "Not mad, sweetie, just ticked OFF!" Somehow my voice had taken on a life of its own, creating its very own crescendo.

And Stephie jumped back in response to it, spilling milk all over herself. And I mean all over.

"Oh, great! Hurry, somebody get some towels!" Then I began to shriek for Stan, who had not yet made his morning appearance. "Get your tail out here and help me!" It wasn't just any plea, it was a full command.

Of course, Stan didn't appear on cue. Not our too-good-to-lift-a-finger-when-most-needed eldest sibling. Nope. He sauntered into the kitchen a good three minutes later, while Carrie, Stephie, and I were down on our hands and knees mopping up the floor with bath towels from upstairs—with a little help from Goofey, too.

"Mom's gonna have a cow if you don't get this milky smell out of her good towels," Carrie informed me.

"It wasn't my idea to use the best ones in the house," I shot back. "Besides, you know where the washing machine is, I do believe."

She got the message and whined as she went. Carrie carried the drippy, milky towels, all rolled up in the largest mixing bowl I could find, downstairs to the laundry room.

"Whew, what a morning!" I said, trying to avoid eye contact with Stan as I stood up.

He was tiptoeing around the yucky floor, heading for the dining room with a bowl of dry cereal in hand. "We all out of milk?" he had the nerve to ask.

I didn't even justify his stupidity with an answer. The guy was a wash-up! As a stepbrother ... shoot, as a human being!

Turning my attention to Stephie, I guided her back upstairs to the bathroom, where she began to undress. I drew some warm bathwater to expedite things.

"Will I be late for school?" she asked tearfully.

"Not if I can help it."

"Will you write a note for my teacher if I am?" she pleaded.

I thought about that. Did I have the right to do such a thing? "We'll see," I said, attempting to reassure her. "Maybe Daddy'll come home and surprise us. I'm sure he'll be needing a warm shower and a change of clothes this morning."

She smiled. The thought of her dad showing up on a hectic school morning must've warmed her heart. I know it did mine. And as it turned out, Uncle Jack made it home in time to kiss all of us good-bye.

"We've got us a new baby." He beamed.

I wanted to ask if maybe, just maybe, I could possibly start thinking about packing for the choir trip tomorrow—that maybe he and Stan could alternate running the family until next Tuesday when Mrs. Duncan and our show choir flew back home to Dressel Hills.

But, no, I was overcome with shyness and a bit of dread, and not wanting to confront Stan with my brain wave right in front of our dad, I kept my mouth shut and went off to school.

ELEVEN

Andie was a whirlwind of chatter when I caught up with her in the hall. "What's the deal?" she asked, almost demanding an answer. "I mean, your mom's had her baby, so what's keeping you here?"

"It's complicated." I sighed, not wanting to rehash things.

She stared at me, wrinkling up her face. "I don't get it, what's the problem?"

"Let's just say: Be glad, be very glad, you and Stan broke up last summer."

"Huh?" Her face wore a giant frown. "Holly, you're not making a bit of sense."

"Take it from me, he would be an unfit husband if you and he ever ended up married. And that's all I'm saying." I turned to go.

"Whoa there, girl. What's this about?"

I glanced back at her, spouting over my shoulder. "Stan's the key. He's the reason I can't go."

"Stan?" She was running after me now. "Why him?"

"The boy's got no sense of responsibility," I spouted. "He refuses to help at home. I'm stuck here, because I'm the only mature offspring presently able to handle things for my parents."

She stopped with me at my locker. "What if I had a little talk with Stan?"

Shaking my head, I made her vow not to breathe a word. "Don't you dare. He's already a royal pain, and if you start hammering away at the shoulds and shouldn'ts of his life, it'll just cause more trouble for me."

She reluctantly agreed. "When will you know if you're going or not?"

"As it stands this minute, it's been decided—I'm not."

"So"—her dark eyes grew wide and she twisted a curl with her pointer finger—"are you saying we have one day to turn this whole thing around?"

Leave it to Andie. I hugged her hard. Never, ever had there been a better friend.

Suddenly, I remembered the promise Uncle Jack had made on the phone earlier. "I'll work on Uncle Jack," I said, "if you'll pray . . . really pray!"

"And you're positive I shouldn't say anything to Stan?"

"Absolutely." I fumbled for some coins in my

wallet. "I have to make a quick call." I dashed off to the pay phone near the school entrance.

"You have reached the residence of a very proud father," Uncle Jack said first thing.

"Hey, that's a nice touch." I laughed.

"Holly? Is everything all right at school?"

"Sure is." Now that I had him on the line, I didn't know how to begin or what to say.

"Something on your mind?" he asked.

I said it. Came right out and asked, "Did you talk to Stan this morning about, uh . . ."

"Oh, that, yes, I intend to sit him down after school, probably sometime tonight."

Tonight? Too late.

"Oh."

"Well, if that's all you called about, kiddo, I'm real anxious to get back to the hospital."

"Okay, well, 'bye." I hung up. Nothing had been settled. I'd have to tell Andie that things looked bleaker than ever. As far as I could see, it would take a miracle for me to be on the plane to Washington, D.C.

Tomorrow.

❤   ❤   ❤

I was attempting to follow one of Mom's outstanding recipes for chicken and rice when the phone rang.

Carrie caught it on the first half of the ring. "Meredith-Patterson funny farm," I heard her say from the kitchen.

"Carrie!" I reprimanded, only to witness a

76

stream of giggles. My sister was definitely puberty-bound.

"It's for you," she called.

"Who is it?"

"Andie—she needs you." She peeked around the corner of the dining room, making a smirk.

I washed and dried my greasy hands. "I'll take it out here," I informed her and picked up the portable phone.

"How's kitchen duty?" Andie joked when I answered.

"Very funny."

"Any news?"

"About?"

"You know . . . has anything happened yet?" she asked, all too eager to hear an affirmative answer.

"Well, for starters, Stan's in his room and Uncle Jack's not home yet, so I really don't know."

"I suggest you do your laundry and start packing, just in case," she advised. "You never know what might happen."

"I can just imagine what might happen. The house could burn down and the children go hungry if Stan's in charge. You know, I'm actually starting to think maybe I should just stay put."

"Holly! How can you say that?"

I went to the archway between the kitchen and the dining room and poked my head in, scouring for snoopers. And sure enough, Carrie was sitting, knees squashed up to her chin, under the table—eyes wide.

"Excuse me a second, Andie," I said, making a big deal about this, even though I wasn't really that upset. I figured I ought to set a precedent since I was the only one in charge at the moment. I covered the receiver with my hand. "Carrie Meredith—out of there!"

"You sound like a mean mommy," she wailed.

"And I'll be dishing out extra chores like some moms do, too, if you don't watch your mouth."

"I'm sorry," she sputtered.

"I could use some help in the kitchen," I told her. "But give me five minutes."

She nodded compliantly and headed upstairs.

"Andie," I said, returning to the phone. "Okay, now I can talk. Where were we? Oh, yes . . . about packing and stuff."

"Why not?" she insisted. "Remember, Sean's expecting to see you."

She didn't have to remind me. "Which brings me to something," I added. "I want you to give him a message for me—you know, explain why I couldn't come."

"So . . . you're giving up? Well, I'm not going to pass on any secondhand information," she said. "You're going on choir auditions, and that's final!"

"Please, Andie, you're blowing this out of proportion," I said. "It's not that I don't want to go, I do. But what would you do if you were me?"

"It wouldn't be easy, that's for sure. But like I said at school, now that your mom's had the baby, why can't your stepdad help out?"

I shrugged. Did I dare ask him?

"Please just think about talking to him?" she pleaded.

"Well, if he doesn't come home too tired, maybe I will."

"Too tired?" Andie was beside herself. "You can't just let this go. Maybe I should come over there."

"No, no. That's not a good idea."

So, once again, I thought things were sorta settled. At least about what step I should take next.

❤   ❤   ❤

I never even heard Uncle Jack come home.

By the time I fussed and fought with Carrie, and later with Stan (because he couldn't seem to work it out to take us to the hospital to see the baby), I was exhausted. And feeling blue.

I had a very suspicious feeling that Stan was actually putting off seeing our new sister. For some strange, probably macho, reason.

Mark and Phil were much easier to handle than the girls, and when I told them to clean up their rooms after supper and do their homework, they did it. I was shocked.

Fortunately, I had less homework than usual. I headed for my room and started working, only to find that I had fallen asleep at my desk!

When I looked at the clock, it was midnight.

Oh, no, I thought. *I've completely lost my chance!*

And sure enough, when I tiptoed down the hall to see if Uncle Jack was home, I spotted his bathrobe lying at the foot of the bed. And, listening for a moment, I heard snoring.

Uncle Jack was home ... and I'd missed him!

Sad and desperate, I headed downstairs for some milk and cookies. The burden of responsibility had already begun to lessen somewhat, just having an adult back in the house, especially at night. But knowing what I was about to miss out on made me angry.

There was plenty of milk in the fridge—a whole gallon. I reached for it, thankful for a man like Uncle Jack in our lives. Even without a grocery list, he'd taken it upon himself to remember a few of the basic food groups consumed in this house.

Slowly, I poured a glass of milk.

Glancing down, I noticed Goofey. "Didja come to keep a lonely girl company?" I picked him up.

He purred, eyeing my glass. "All right," I said, putting him down and getting his bowl. "If I'm up, you have to be up, too ... is that it?"

Goofey meowed.

Then I heard a sound in the dining room and turned to see Uncle Jack coming toward the kitchen. "What's this? A midnight snack?" He grinned. "Mind if I join you?"

"Okay."

He sat on a bar stool and leaned forward on his elbow. "Guess I should've wakened you earlier."

"That's fine," I said, glad to have this opportunity, at least. "I think I was probably wiped out."

"It certainly looked that way to me. And I must

say, not a very good way for a young lady to start out on an important trip."

I turned away from the cookie jar and stared at him. I'd scarcely been listening at this point, thinking he was just coming downstairs to chitchat or have a snack. But this—what had he just said?

"I'm sorry, could you repeat that?" I held my breath.

"I've got you covered, Holly-Heart," he said with a broad grin. "You're going to Washington, D.C."

I ran to him, and stifling a shriek of joy, I hugged the daylights out of him.

"Now, then, do you need help getting ready?" he asked.

"Well, I'll just do a quick load of laundry if it's all right." I was fully awake, adrenaline rushing through my veins!

He nodded his approval.

"Oh, thank you, Uncle Jack," I said again. "I hope this isn't going to be a hardship on you."

"Not at all. And Stan's going to have a golden opportunity to learn firsthand what family life's all about."

"Stan?" I gulped. "He's going to be in charge?"

"Not totally. But he'll be in training of sorts, that's for certain."

"In training?"

"Yes, Miss Hibbard has agreed to oversee things before and after school, till I can get home from work."

I laughed out loud. "Our next-door neighbor? You're kidding! Does Stan know about this?"

"He knows, and he'll just have to live with it."

I chuckled, heading upstairs to think through the items of clothing and things I needed for my trip. Miss Hibbard, the pickiest little old lady in Dressel Hills, was going to whip Stan Patterson into shape!

Was this justice or what?

TWELVE

I had only one regret about leaving my family behind: Not getting to lay eyes on my baby sister before I left.

Mrs. Duncan was overjoyed about my coming. So was Andie. And if I'm not too presumptuous to say so, I think Jared Wilkins looked very pleased, too.

I, however, could hardly contain myself as we filed into the coach section of the airplane. "You'll never believe what I was doing at one o'clock this morning," I said, settling into the aisle seat next to Andie.

"Dirty laundry?" She laughed. "I told you, and you didn't listen!"

"Well, for once, you were right." I stuffed my carry-on bag beneath the seat directly in front of me, still wiggling with excitement, not to mention the effects of several glasses of pop.

Uncle Jack would've surely freaked if he'd known what I'd had to drink for breakfast. But adrenaline doesn't last forever, and when you've had only a few hours' sleep, well . . .

The shuttle flight to Denver lasted about forty minutes, and then all of us experienced the fun of finding our way (and trying to stay together) through the maze of concourses and underground shuttles at Denver International Airport.

But soon we were seated in the waiting area ready for the Boeing 737 to fly us to Chicago. There, we'd be changing planes again.

"What will you do when you see Sean?" asked Andie right out of the blue.

"Run up to him, throw my arms around him, and give him a big pucker." I chuckled sarcastically. "What do you think I'll do, silly?"

"Hey, I was serious."

"So was I." We giggled about it, and when we'd calmed down a bit, I told her that I was actually feeling awkward about meeting Sean again, especially with the whole choir hanging around.

"Ah, it's nothing, right? You're just friends."

I shook my head at her. She had me good.

"So . . . I'm right, there is more to the Sean Hamilton-Holly Meredith story."

"Not really."

"Uh-huh." And she rolled her eyes at me.

❤   ❤   ❤

Chicago's O'Hare International Airport was bustling with people coming and going, and although we didn't have to rush off to catch our connecting flight, I could see that it was difficult for Mrs. Duncan and the three adult sponsors to keep track of us. We were like sheep being herded—all twenty-five of us.

But even as we waited to go down the escalator, I couldn't help thinking about my new sister back home.

Shoot, I hadn't even had a chance to say "thanks" to Mom before I left. And I was pretty sure she was responsible for my getting to come at the last minute. I decided to call her once we got settled in our hotel.

One by one, we stepped onto the moving walkway in the underground level, surrounded by the coolest neon and strobe light show ever.

"What do you think, Holly?" Jared called back to me. "Check out what you would've missed."

"It's fabulous," I replied, watching a chartreuse-orange design blink off the wall.

"Sure is!" Andie poked my back.

Paula crowded in from behind. "Who's your baby sister look like?"

"Uncle Jack says she's a charmer, but since I haven't seen her yet, I really don't know."

"You haven't seen her?" Kayla said, all aghast. "Why not?"

"It's a long story," I explained. "Beginning with an S and ending with an N."

That's all that needed to be said. She figured it

out, especially with Andie's help—who turned around, mouthing nasties about Stan.

"Well, I guess you *are* lucky to be here," Paula said.

"Considering everything, yeah," I replied.

❤   ❤   ❤

That night, I wrote in my journal.
Friday, April 19th
I can't believe it! Several times during the flight, I pinched myself to make sure it wasn't just a glorious dream.

We're staying in this magnificent, old, historic hotel. (We're getting a special rate, because there are so many of us.) From the penthouse, Andie, Paula, Kayla, and I checked out the Mall in the distance—what a view! It's not a shopping mall, though. It's a park—a wide, grassy carpet—two miles long, running between the Washington Monument and Capitol Hill.

This evening, after we checked into the hotel, we went to the John F. Kennedy Center for the Performing Arts building—it's huge, made of marble, and surrounded by pillars. Oh, yes ... it overlooks the Potomac River. This is where we'll audition tomorrow afternoon.

I'm so excited ... nervous, too. So is everyone else. Mrs. Duncan has been great about soothing our fears, encouraging us with her "we-can-do-it" comments. Still, it's frazzling. I mean, here we are. We made districts, state, and regionals. And the best of the best are competing along with us.

Do we have what it takes to win?

I packed my journal-notebook back into the bottom of my suitcase. Of course, I knew I could trust my girlfriends. It wasn't like being back home with two little snoopers scoping out every tiny tidbit of my life.

When the twins finished talking to their parents, I dialed the operator for assistance. He put me through to Dressel Hills General Hospital. Two thousand miles away!

"Mom, hi ... it's me, Holly."

"Oh, honey, you're there already?" She sounded a little drugged up.

"It's two hours later here."

"That's right." She yawned. "I hope you and your friends are having a good time."

"Yes, but how are you?"

"Still a bit groggy."

"How's the baby?" I asked.

"Aw, April's so sweet and pretty. She's all ready to go home, but we're stuck here another couple days."

"That's probably good, Mom. Take your time getting your strength back, okay?" I didn't want to tell her that she should stay in the hospital as long as possible. What awaited her at 207 Downhill Court would discourage any surgery patient!

I kept talking. "I didn't get a chance to thank you for talking Uncle Jack into letting me come."

"Oh, he didn't talk me into it. Your brother did."

"Who?"

"Stan called last night, sometime after supper, I

think. He said you were dying to go with the choir."

"He said that?"

"He certainly did, and when Jack and I talked it over, we decided to call on Miss Hibbard to supervise."

"Wow, I had no idea that Stan—"

"Yes, you have your stepbrother to thank for this," she said again, beginning to sound a bit droopy. I had a feeling she was going to fall asleep on me.

"Well, I hope you're feeling better real soon, Mom. I love you."

"Love you, too."

"Good-bye. And give April a kiss for me."

"I will."

When I hung up, I told Andie and the twins what Mom had said about Stan. "Can you figure this?"

"Maybe Stan isn't as horrid as you think," Kayla spoke up. But, of course, she didn't really count. Because she'd been sweet on him since day one.

"He's horrid, all right," I stated. "It's just that he got tired of hearing me hound about shirking his duty. That's gotta be it."

"Well . . . maybe." Andie had a sly smile on her face.

"Wait a minute." I grabbed a pillow and flung it at her. "Did you have something to do with this?"

"Me? I promised . . . remember?" Her eyes told another story.

"Andie, how am I ever gonna trust you?" I said, laughing.

"I got you right here, girl—didn't I?"

The answer to that was a perfectly fabulous pillow fight—minus a zillion feathers. Nope. These state-of-the-art hotel pillows were the absolute best around.

Hopefully, so was the Dressel Hills Show Choir.

THIRTEEN

I don't remember encountering air as anticipation-thick as it was the next afternoon. Right after lunch, no less! Everyone in the choir felt it, too. I could see it on their faces—the brightness, the urgency. The desire to sing to our utmost ability.

We used our allotted time to vocalize, but as warmed up and mellow as we sounded, there were still a few "bugs" to work out. Things like confidence and poise—all-important elements. And, if missing, were sure to stand out!

Since we didn't want to look like hicks from the sticks—not here, surrounded by all the grandeur of the nation's capital—we listened carefully as Mrs. Duncan gave us our final "polishing."

"She's fine-tuning us again," Andie said, referring to our director.

I grinned back at my friend. "Yep, Mrs. Duncan is the best."

Lined up and waiting in the wings, we agonized through the fabulous sounds of two other choirs ahead of us. One group hailed from West Virginia, not far from here. The other choir was an all-black, all-girl choir from New York City. After hearing their performance, I was worried. These babes were out-of-this-world-good, and there was no getting around it—we were up against style and charisma—a total class act!

I caught Mrs. Duncan's eye and shrugged during the audience applause. Promptly, she poked up her thumb and flashed a plucky grin. She believed in us.

And ... we were next.

The emcee was introducing us as we crept over the silent, velvety floor behind the main curtains. "And now, from colorful Colorado, I give you the Dressel Hills High School Show Choir!"

Of course the audience was jazzed—the last group had wound them up. Anyway, we were greeted with a thunderous welcome. And when the side curtains parted automatically, we walked onto the stage, single file, finding our way to our appointed spots on the risers.

There was no seeing the audience, because the spotlights on us were so hot and bright. Somewhere, out in the sea of blackness, the Miller twins' relatives were watching ... along with the vice president of the United States!

I don't know why, but once we stood there, I

realized how very high these risers were compared to the ones back home. For a split second, I thought I might become dizzy and, heaven forbid, pass out in front of half the population of . . .

It was déjà vu—recalling a scene from another time and another place—our seventh grade musical, two years back. I could even hear a familiar voice saying, "Holly Meredith, you're green!" But I shoved the ridiculous thought out of my mind.

Mrs. Duncan gave a cue for Andie to play the four-note chord, which started us off on our a cappella madrigals. Thank goodness, the illusion was gone, and I focused hard on remembering my part—along with each of my choir-member friends.

We sang from our hearts. No question.

Mrs. Duncan's face reflected our enthusiasm, and the coolest thing—we sounded great!

After the audition, we left the stage via another magical portal, unseen by the audience. This was the stuff of fairy tales, and once all of us were in the same place again, we were given a tour of the building. We saw six beautiful theatres housed inside the center. My favorites were the Eisenhower Theatre, mainly for plays, and the Terrace Theatre, where people from all over the world come to experience poetry readings, modern dance, and drama.

I couldn't help wondering what it would be like to play Maria Von Trapp—female lead for *The Sound of Music*—on one of those incredible stages.

Next, we took the Metro, an underground subway system, with the coolest curved and indented walls and roof—reminding me of Mom's Saturday-morning waffles. Only these were warped!

Lincoln Memorial, next stop. Everyone, it seemed, had to have individual pictures taken in front of Lincoln's huge statue—nineteen feet high! Tears came to my eyes as I read the opening lines of the Gettysburg Address, etched in marble. "Four score and seven years ago . . ."

What a place!

Mrs. Duncan gathered all of us for a group shot. Before we disbanded, she asked, "How many want to see Ford's Theatre? We still have time."

It was unanimous.

"Anyone tired?" she asked.

No one would admit it. We were in fabulous Washington, D.C., for pete's sake!

Andie, Paula, and I stuck together. Kayla and Amy-Liz were close behind us when we caught the Metro again. Soon we were being whisked downtown . . . and back in time.

The old theater on Tenth Street had been restored to its appearance on that fateful night in 1865, when Abraham Lincoln had been fatally shot. During the story of the assassination—dramatically told by the guide—Andie literally jumped at the shot of the blank gun.

Exhausted, but delighted with the events of the day, we headed to the nearest pizza place for supper.

❤   ❤   ❤

"How'd the audition go?" Uncle Jack asked later that evening, when I called the hospital.

"Mrs. Duncan says we were great."

"What's the Kennedy Center like?" he asked.

"Perfect. I think it must be acoustically flawless. I mean, not only could we hear our voices coming through the giant stage speakers, we actually got the feel of the auditorium, even though it was so huge. It's an incredible place." I sighed. "I don't know, I guess it's hard to put into words."

He chuckled a bit. "I guess that's how you might describe the little dumplin' I have here in my arms. You couldn't begin to describe *her* with words."

"Aw . . . you must be holding April," I cooed.

"Just a minute, the whole family's here for a visit." He gave the phone to Mom.

"Hi, Holly-Heart. Sounds like the audition went well." She sounded pretty well, herself.

"I wish you could've heard us sing," I said.

"Oh, I'm so happy for you, honey."

There was mumbling going on in the background—someone was telling Stan to sit down with the baby.

I almost cracked up. "What's Stan doing?"

"Oh, he asked to hold his baby sister," Mom explained. "And I don't think he quite remembers how. It's been a long time since Stephie was tiny."

"For sure," I muttered, but I was confused. I really couldn't picture it. Stan—holding a two-day-old infant?

Carrie got on the line next. "Hey, Holly, I think

94

you got something from that publisher person—
you know, the one in Chicago?"

"Really? What's the writing look like?"

"Huh?"

"The address, on the envelope—whose writing
is it?" I knew if it were mine—the self-addressed,
stamped envelope—it was a definite rejection.

"I think it was typewritten," she replied.

"Large or small envelope?"

"Small."

"Yes!" This was so fabulous. I couldn't wait to
tell Jared.

Briefly, I talked to Mom again, then said good-
bye. But even as I hung up the phone, I could not
conjure up the image of Stan holding baby April!

When I told my roommates about it, they broke
into hilarious laughter. None of them could believe
it—especially not Andie. Kayla, yeah, because, like
I said, she had this major thing for my brousin.

Andie had ordered room service, of all things.
"It's part of the deal, right?" she said, laughing it
off.

"It's not like we have carte blanche," I reprimanded her. "This stuff is expensive, and the tax-
payers of Dressel Hills aren't picking up the tab.
We're on our own."

Paula nodded. "Which reminds me, Mrs.
Duncan said to go easy on expenditures."

"No kidding." I stared at Andie.

She whipped out a couple twenties and waved

them around. "Maybe, but my dad said I could live it up . . . just a little."

It turned out, she'd ordered root-beer floats for all of us. When? Who knows. But I have a sneaking suspicion it was while Paula, Kayla, and I went exploring the pool room and spa. Right after we got back.

Anyway, we slurped them up, found an old black-and-white movie on cable TV, and snuggled down for a night of girl-talk and giggling.

Two hours later, Andie gasped, clutching her throat. Honestly, I thought she was choking. "You haven't called Sean yet, have you?"

I grinned. "Wouldn't you like to know?"

"Holly! C'mon—don't forget who's responsible for getting you here."

"Uh-huh." I grinned back at her.

She leaped onto my bed, followed by Kayla and Paula. "So tell us, is the love of your life coming with us Monday?"

There was no keeping it quiet any longer. "He's joining us for the FBI tour, and it looks like he'll be able to hang out with us most of the day."

"With us?" Andie teased. "C'mon, Holly, we all know it's you he wants to see."

I shrugged, thinking they were probably right. Only thing, how would Sean fit into the group dynamics here? After having established a comfortable letter-writing friendship, well, I just didn't know how things would work out. I guess I'd find out.

Sooner or later.

FOURTEEN

Sunday morning, our choir performed two sacred numbers at two different churches in the downtown area. Most of the regional finalists had been scheduled to do the same thing around town.

One of the locations turned out to be where the president and first lady attended church. Man, did we go through major security rigmarole before entering! But it was definitely worth it to look out into the crowd, while singing, and see their familiar faces.

Later, after lunch, we sat in on several more auditions at the Kennedy Center. Relaxing there beneath one of the dazzling chandeliers, I honestly wondered how the judges could ever begin to choose a grand winner. Every group sounded fabulous.

Andie, however, was partial to the ensembles with piano accompaniment. Personally, I liked a cappella better. Maybe because there was something terribly ethereal and natural about the sound of pure, unaccompanied voices. Anyway, sitting out in the spectacular auditorium sent shivers up my spine. And it whet my appetite for tonight's supper-theater entertainment to come.

❤   ❤   ❤

Somehow, Jared landed a seat next to me at the table that evening. I was glad, though. It was the perfect opportunity to discuss the status of my manuscript. "I think there might be something waiting for me at home—a response about the story I sent to your uncle."

"Your novella?"

I nodded. "If Carrie's right, I might have an acceptance letter."

He grinned. "Bet you're right."

"You know about it?" I stared at him, incredulously.

He filled me in on the details, and as it turned out, his short story had also been chosen for publication.

"Once again, we'll be published together," I said, remembering the story he'd written under a female pen name—for a girl's magazine, no less!

"Yeah." He gave my arm a teeny squeeze, and even though a bunch of kids from choir witnessed the gesture, I didn't mind. Jared was actually okay!

♥ ♥ ♥

The next morning, at eight o'clock, Sean linked up with us as we waited on E Street for a tour of the J. Edgar Hoover FBI Building. I spotted his blonde crew cut first off, and after being nudged nearly out of line by giggly Andie, I called to him.

Sean came right over, almost sprinting. I was surprised to see how much taller he was—and really tan. "Hi, Holly. It's good to see you again." His smile was warm and endearing.

"Same here," I said, trying to tune out the running dialogue between Andie and the twins—behind me. "I'd like you to meet some of my friends."

I spotted Mrs. Duncan ahead of us and led Sean over to meet our choir director and the adult sponsors. I could tell Andie was having a fit about it by the way she glared at me as we got back in line a few minutes later.

To appease her, I reintroduced Sean to her. "I'm sure you remember Andie Martinez."

He extended his hand like a true gentleman. "Hey, Andie. How's it going?"

While I was introducing Paula and Kayla, Jared happened to come over. "This is Jared Wilkins," I told Sean. Then turning to Jared, I said, "I'd like you to meet my California friend, Sean Hamilton."

The two of them shook hands, too, Jared taking the initiative and striking up a conversation with Sean. I was terribly impressed at Jared's maturity as I observed them together. He'd come a long way since his "jealousy days"!

Soon, the long line of eager tourists began to move. Mrs. Duncan informed us that this was the week for the White House spring garden tour. "That's why America's hometown is overcrowded with sightseers," she explained.

Personally, I was glad the auditions had been held this month. I couldn't begin to imagine what Washington, D.C., would be like in summer with school out.

Sean fell in step with me, and we talked about his cross-continental flight and what had happened so far with the choir auditions. "A decision will be made by tonight," I told him. "The first-place winning choir gets to sing at the Capitol, in the rotunda tomorrow at noon."

"Cool." He grinned. "In front of lots of congressmen?"

"And women."

He laughed. "Of course!"

Soon, we were led through the entrance to the block-long building—the John Dillinger "death mask" and the "Ten Most Wanted" list exhibits greeted us. A gripping crime show!

Danny Myers and some of the other guys asked questions, but the guide wasn't stumped by any of them. In fact, he seemed to have an answer for everything, along with additional stories—complete with blood-curdling details.

Sean, who was pursuing a career in medicine,

was most interested in the crime labs, where technicians did all sorts of scrutinizing work. Things like analyzing handwriting and fibers and determining blood types.

Next, we were taken to a room filled with over four thousand guns and twelve thousand different kinds of ammunition. Some of the guys in the group got overtly macho suddenly, but not Sean. He listened and observed, like the gentleman he was.

Last, but not least, we witnessed the FBI's very own indoor firing range—noisy and action-packed. Personally, I was glad to get out of there!

After the FBI tour, we caught the Metrorail, which sped us away to the National Air and Space Museum. Mrs. Duncan told us before we ever stepped inside that this was the most-visited museum in the world. About eight million people visited each year!

When our group was divided in half by our adult sponsors, Andie smirked about it—which meant she wasn't thrilled about her and the Miller twins being separated from Sean and me. I figured she'd get over it. Besides, it was a much better arrangement . . . for my guy friend and me.

The place was literally soaring with airplanes, rockets, and missiles—from the Wright brothers' 1903 "Flyer" to the Viking Mars Lander. I had a hard time keeping up with our small group, though, because I really wanted to just stand and gawk at each exhibit. And the space probes and satellites floating overhead.

"C'mon, Holly," Sean called to me once. "I'd hate to see you 'space out' in here."

I laughed. "You're pun-ny," I said about his play on words. And he was. A real wit and a half!

About an hour later, while we were exploring the huge Skylab space station, suddenly our group vanished. It seemed so weird, especially because just seconds before, we'd all been together—right here in this huge silver barrel-shaped orbital workshop.

"If we hurry, maybe we can track 'em down," Sean suggested.

So we rushed down the long middle hall, trying to spot anyone familiar. We even backtracked through each of the two-story hallways, searching everywhere.

After checking the Albert Einstein Planetarium section, we decided it was futile; besides, we didn't want to waste valuable sight-seeing time. We would go it alone. And secretly, I was thrilled!

"I hope Mrs. Duncan and the others won't worry," I said as we made our way outside, into the warm, bright sunshine.

"Oh, there's a good chance we'll run into them," Sean assured me. "Any idea where they'd be headed next?"

"Probably somewhere for lunch, but beats me where."

I really wasn't sure about the best approach to take—about locating our group. Neither did Sean, but he had a great idea. "Let's grab a snack. I don't know about you, but I'm starved."

We walked to a hot dog stand one block away. While we waited in line, Sean and I talked—mostly about the monuments and the attractions. But what I really wanted to know were his impressions of George Washington University and the college day activities over the past weekend. But I decided not to be nosy—I'd wait till he brought it up.

With the sun shining down on us through newly formed leaves, Sean asked, "What's your favorite attraction so far?"

"It's hard to say," I replied, telling him about the splendor of the Lincoln Memorial and the drama of Ford's Theatre. "We saw those yesterday." I paused for moment. "What I really think I liked best was the space museum—touching the moon rock was so cool. What about you?"

"Has to be the FBI building."

I wasn't surprised. The place was perfect for a guy interested in blood, hearts, and medical stuff.

We were finally close enough to the food stand to read the prices—three times higher than in Dressel Hills—probably any other place in the world, too.

"How hungry are you?" he asked with a grin.

"A little." But I certainly didn't want him to think he had to pay for me. Quickly, I pulled out my wallet. The face of George Washington on my one-dollar bills, gave me an idea. "Hey, wanna visit the Bureau of Engraving and Printing this afternoon? My stepdad highly recommended it."

Sean promptly found his tourist guide and map. "Sounds like fun. I hear they print more than 18 million bills every day."

I was surprised at how agreeable he was. Of course, Andie would say he was only trying to impress me. But I had a different take on the way Sean handled himself around a young lady, namely me. It had nothing to do with trying to sway or influence me. Nope. Sean was a well-bred, very nice, Christian guy.

And I secretly hoped our friendship might continue for a long time. At least, until he and I came to know God's romantic plans for our lives. Of course, no way would I discuss the book I'd read recently. Not with Sean! I wouldn't want him to think I was bold, or, as my mother called it—forward. According to her, if you want to attract a nice boy, never, ever chase him.

Surprisingly enough, I'd found this to be true in the past. The best way to attract friendships with boys was to allow them to do the pursuing.

And over hot dogs, fries smothered in ketchup, and a lot of pop, I let Sean do just that.

FIFTEEN

Sean did end up paying for my lunch, even though I told him I was quite capable of handling my own financial affairs.

Of course, he wouldn't hear of it. So, I guess I could actually say this had just been my very first real date—even though I'd tried to convince myself that I wasn't interested in the formal dating thing much anymore.

Mom had made this rule years ago, that I had to be fifteen to go out on an actual date with a guy. Oh sure, I'd spent lots of time in groups with boys from our church, but for some reason, I'd built up this whole date-thing in my mind. Built it way up! Longing, waiting for the second I turned fifteen.

Funny thing, though. My thinking had begun to change, partly because of that cool book, and for another reason, too. Sean was my good friend. The way I saw it, our relationship was fabulous—and absolutely appropriate for our age—just the way it was. To think of him in a romantic, gushy sense would surely spoil things. I couldn't risk anything happening to the beautiful rapport we shared.

So, I was determined to shove out the first-date notion and focus on simply sharing and listening to my friend.

After lunch we walked nearly three blocks on the grassy strip called the Mall, toward the Bureau of Engraving and Printing. Ordinary sights and sounds captured our attention along the way—little kids from a day care having a picnic and a group of older folk on bicycles.

We soaked up the gentle, warm breezes of a romantic April afternoon ... er, I mean a friendly one.

Finally, I couldn't wait any longer. I simply had to ask the question burning inside me. "What do you think of the university here?" I blurted.

Sean smiled as we walked, glancing at me as if he might be ready to discuss it. "I want to check out two others before I make my final decision. You know, take my time about it."

"So you're not that wild about George Washington University?"

"It's really great—but too far away from California."

"Where are the other schools?" I asked, genuinely interested.

"One's KU—Kansas University." He paused for a moment, a wide grin spreading across his face. "And the other is CU—Colorado University in Boulder, Colorado."

"You're kidding! You might go to school in *my* state?"

He stopped walking and turned to me. "Wouldn't it be great, Holly? And so handy for me to see you more often."

"That would be fun," I admitted as a curious feeling caught me by surprise.

I was glad it was his turn to ask questions. "Any idea where you might go to school?"

We resumed our walk, the smell of daffodils in the air. Letting my hair blow freely, I told him some of my future aspirations. "Well, I'm really interested in becoming a published book author ... someday. It's hard to say what school I should attend for that sort of thing. I know I want to study plenty of English and American literature before I attempt a novel or anything serious. Besides, Mrs. Ross, my English teacher, says a writer needs to live and experience life for a while before attempting a book."

Sean listened with rapt attention. In fact, both of us were so caught up in conversation, we almost missed turning south at Fourteenth Street.

"What are the chances of your show choir taking first place?" Sean asked later as we waited for the next available tour in front of the gray building— where America's paper money was printed.

"Well, if you could've heard the other groups audition, you might think we had zero chance."

"Really? Which ones were best?"

I told him my three top picks—one of them included the all-girls group from New York City. "I guess when it comes right down to it, we'll have to trust the judges' vote." I shook my head. "Man, I'd hate to be the one picking!"

He stepped back a bit, studying me. "What if— just what if—your choir is chosen? When would you be going to Austria for international auditions?"

"Why do you want to know?" I wondered what he was really asking.

"Is it this summer?" he persisted.

"Sometime in mid-June, I think."

And by the way he nearly chuckled, I had a funny feeling he was fishing for something.

"C'mon," I pleaded. "What's up?"

"Let's just see if your choir wins or not." That's all he would say.

I was beginning to feel comfortable with him. Really comfortable. That's when I brought up the subject of the book I'd read, and I wasn't being forward about it either. "It's really incredible—the concepts in it, I mean."

"Who's the author?" he asked. "It sounds familiar."

I began to tell him about the book. Afterwards, I hoped I'd done the right thing. "So, what do you think?" I asked, noting a sign warning tourists about taking flash photography. "Is it a radical idea?"

"There'd sure be a lot less broken hearts in the world."

I agreed. And I didn't tell him, but from past experience, I knew that the minute I let a boy hold my hand, the relationship had already begun to change. Physical attraction would become the bigger interest. Even bigger than the friendship.

We talked more about it, and soon, he was pulling out his wallet and asking me for the name of the author. I waited while he jotted it down, inching along with the crowd.

At last, we were inside and listening to an informative, but brief, spiel on the production of currency. How it was designed, engraved, and printed. Progressing along, we watched as thousands of dollars zipped through the printing presses. There were forklifts hauling crisp, green dollar bills, and other interesting things to see, like tons of postage stamps and passports.

Seeing the passports made me think of Sean's secretive comment. Why did he want to know about Austria? Was he going there this summer?

Well into the tour, Sean leaned over, and before I could stop him, he aimed his camera and flashed.

"Halt right there, young man!" a deep voice bellowed into the crowd. The burly guard whipped out his two-way radio and began reporting the infraction as he headed straight for us!

Tugging on Sean's shirtsleeve, I said, "Didn't you

see the sign back there?" I was sure he hadn't. But that didn't seem to hinder the guard.

"Hand over that camera!" the stern command was given.

I cringed. Was my friend going to jail?

"It's against the law to take pictures in a federal building." The guard was obviously wired up.

"I'm very sorry, sir," Sean spoke up. "I didn't see any sign, otherwise I would've kept my camera in its case."

I worried that Sean's expensive camera might be confiscated—his precious film destroyed.

"How could you miss seeing the signs?" the guard demanded, now out of breath and surveying Sean's camera. "They're posted everywhere."

Sean glanced at me and said tenderly, "I was lost in conversation with my girlfriend."

That helped. The guard hesitantly returned the camera—backing off. But my heart sure didn't! It was going berserk. And after all our logical, serious talk about the fabulous book.

After all that . . .

Shoot, I was so bewildered by the unexpected comment (about being his girlfriend), that at the end of the tour in the visitor's center, I purchased a bag of shredded money as a souvenir!

What was I thinking?

SIXTEEN

"Do you think we'll ever catch up with Mrs. Duncan and the choir?" I asked, still rather dazed, yet reluctant to end our private talk.

A boyish grin spread across Sean's handsome face. "Let's see the Washington Monument next." He studied his map and discovered it was only a few blocks north of us. "It's not far—look for the park and fifty American flags."

I checked my watch. Two o'clock—still plenty of time.

"Is it true the monument stays open till midnight?" I asked. "A friend of mine once told me he climbed all 898 steps and rode the elevator down at midnight." I didn't tell him the friend was Jared Wilkins, while on summer vacation with his family.

Sean held my hand briefly as we crossed the

street, but I knew it was only out of concern for my safety. Besides, I wasn't complaining. After all, my own father, now a Christian, had approved of Sean Hamilton right from the start—another one of the important principles taught in the book I'd read.

❤   ❤   ❤

As it turned out, none of the Dressel Hills choir members were anywhere near the tall marble monument or its reflecting pool to the west. But Sean and I had fun riding the elevator to the top. The view was great, too. Exceptionally clear. We could see for a zillion miles in all four directions.

"Just think," I joked, "if we had binoculars, we might be able to find Mrs. Duncan and the choir from up here."

Sean laughed, but I sensed he wasn't all that worried about linking up with the others. Not yet. The day was young. And since we were in the vicinity, we paid a solemn visit to the Vietnam Veterans' Memorial. Sean found his uncle's name on the black granite wall and asked one of the park employees to make a rubbing of the name.

Baskets of flowers and personal letters, along with many other gifts, had been left behind at the wall. People in uniform and others not, stood and cried openly. After a few moments of observing this perpetual, silent, yet emotional drama, I began to have a modest understanding of the pain and loss that comes with war.

Sean and I walked back to the reflecting pool, deep in thought. There, we sat on the grass and watched the ducks, talking softly about the effects of human cruelty.

After we'd rested our feet, we caught the Tourmobile to the Tomb of the Unknown Soldier and the Eternal Flame at John Kennedy's grave site in Arlington National Cemetery. Sean went camera-crazy, insisting on taking shots of me at each of the famous landmarks—even at some general's gravestone I'd never heard of. Actually, it got to be comical, but I knew it would be a long time before we might see each other again, so I cooperated and put on my best smile for him.

❤   ❤   ❤

Back at the hotel, I waited—actually sacked out on the bed for an hour—before Andie and the twins ever returned. And what a joyful reunion it was!

"We thought you'd eloped or something," Andie joked.

I sat up and blinked my sleepy eyes. "Was Mrs. Duncan worried about us?"

"Not really," Paula chimed in. "Anyone can take one look at Sean and see he's a very responsible guy."

Kayla was nodding her approval. "It was nice, probably, that it worked out this way ... right?"

"If you're saying, did I plan it? Well, I didn't."

"But if you could do it over again, would you get lost again? That's the real question." Andie was being silly. But she was right, and I knew it.

Somehow or other, it seemed almost providential that Sean and I spend the afternoon together.

"Is he coming tonight?" Paula asked as she plopped onto the bed with an exhausted grunt.

"I hope so." I got up and started brushing my hair. "So ... what do you think of him?" I asked rather sheepishly.

Andie jumped right on it. "Aha! She's a goner— I knew it. We should've brought that dating book along with us on this trip!"

I turned to study my friends. "It's okay, I can take a joke." But I wasn't going to share the intimate thoughts going through my mind. Not now. I had some tall praying to do before I told anyone what I was thinking about Sean Hamilton.

After supper at a Chinese place, we took the Metrorail once again—and for the last time this trip—to the Kennedy Center.

Sean showed up promptly and in time to sit with us. All of us wore our patriotic audition outfits— navy blue skirts and white blouses with red dress ties, in case we were winners.

"You look great," he whispered.

"Thanks, so do you." And I meant it. Sean was a fabulous dresser, wearing cream-colored cotton trousers and a light blue shirt. I was proud to be seen with him. And Mrs. Duncan obviously approved, too, because when I caught her eye, she winked at us.

The announcer started the evening by thanking the many choral groups from around the country. I glanced at Andie and saw that she had her fingers crossed. I hoped she wouldn't be disappointed if we didn't make it. Andie would be talking of nothing else back home, probably for the rest of the school year. On the other hand, if we did win, she'd be packing and planning—shoot, for all of us—between now and June something.

The man in the black tuxedo stood before the microphone, waiting for the echo from the trumpet fanfare to fade completely. "I would like to begin by announcing the winners, starting with second runner-up."

In other words, third place, I thought.

Ceremoniously, he pulled an envelope out of his coat. And we waited as he glanced at the card inside. "Second runner-up, all the way from Oregon—the Portland High School Choralaires!"

Everyone applauded, and I felt myself getting tense. Did we have a chance?

The group from Oregon headed for the stage. They were happy, from the smiles on their faces. They'd get to go to Austria this summer only if the first-place winners and the first runner-up couldn't make it. Phooey. I wouldn't have been smiling!

The emcee continued with his dramatic charade. And . . . I almost missed the most incredible thing! I'd turned to look at Andie and the Miller twins, and the guy started saying something about the choir from Colorado!

What?

I was listening now.

"From the majestic Colorado Rockies—the Dressel Hills Show Choir—our first runner-up!"

Mrs. Duncan motioned for us to stand. Sean was beaming, and I heard him say "Yes!"

I followed the rest of my friends as we headed down the long, carpeted aisle to stand onstage.

Hard as I tried, it was impossible to see Sean's smiling face in the audience as I stood there on the wide, expansive stage. The spotlights were so powerful and the place so charged with excitement, I started to hold my breath again.

"Breathe," Andie said to me over the applause.

And I did. Still, I could hardly believe we were up here. I mean, this was really big-time stuff!

None of us were too surprised when the all-girl choir from New York City took first place. They deserved it as far as I was concerned.

Later, at a glitzy ice cream parlor, Mrs. Duncan congratulated us. "Most likely we won't be going to Vienna in two months, but we've certainly accomplished a worthy goal. I know—and I speak for the principal and all the teachers at Dressel Hills High—you students are absolutely tops. And I'm so very honored to be your director."

Now it was our turn to cheer her! And we did, complete with whistles from some of the guys.

Sean grinned, apparently thrilled to be in the middle of this celebratory commotion. Later, when things died down a bit, and we could actually hear each other without shouting, he told me why he'd asked about Austria earlier. "Your father has some business there this summer," he explained. "He wants me to go along."

"Daddy's going to Europe?" This was the first I'd heard of it.

"I'm going to assist him, I guess you'd say." He smiled. "More as a traveling companion, I suppose."

"Because my stepmom doesn't want to leave Tyler?" He was her young son.

Sean nodded. "Saundra thinks someone should be with your dad because of his heart problems."

I sighed. "Well, lucky you."

He held the door for me as we left the ice cream place. "Who knows, maybe you'll get there yet."

"That would be a miracle—I mean, those New York singers aren't gonna miss out on international competition. No way!"

"Miracles can happen," he replied. And that would have been the last exchange of words between us if it hadn't been for Mrs. Duncan—fabulous teacher she was.

Discreetly, she came over and said the rest of the group would head on to the Metro station if Sean didn't mind escorting me back to the hotel.

"I'd be happy to," he said gallantly.

So the choir and sponsors strolled down the street and out of sight, and for a few moments, we were alone again.

"Thanks for sharing the evening with me," I began. "It was really special." I almost said, "because of you," but didn't. I had a feeling he already knew.

"I wouldn't have missed it for anything, Holly." We looked out over the beautiful Potomac river in the distance. The sky still had a touch of color and light in it. "I wouldn't have missed you."

His words touched my heart. They were trustworthy and good. Just the way he was.

I was almost afraid to look up at him, worried that he might see in my eyes the things I felt.

"Do you mind if I call you long-distance?" he asked. "Is it okay with your family?"

I nodded. "It's fine. I'd like that."

"And we'll write."

"Yes," I whispered, scarcely finding my voice.

We were silent for a moment, listening to the sounds of dusk. Then he said, "Your director is really terrific, you know. Please tell her thanks for me."

I glanced at him, grinning.

He added, "Some teachers might've had a problem about our getting lost today."

"I know what you mean. But Mrs. Duncan's the best."

He reached for my hand unexpectedly. "She's actually quite terrific, but not the best."

I was looking into his face now, no longer bashful. But I was determined not to get emotional. Shoot, I wanted to be able to see this wonderful friend of mine clearly. Besides, tears on a night like this were way overrated!

"Well, I guess this is good-bye," I offered. "Hope you have a good flight home."

"Thanks." He turned to face the river then, our shoulders touching as we looked out toward the sunset. "More sight-seeing tomorrow?"

"We're scheduled to see the White House and the Capitol with our state senator."

He teased, "Watch out for those flash pictures."

"Don't worry." We walked slowly now. "I honestly thought you were going to be hauled off to jail," I said.

He chuckled. "We made some interesting memories together, didn't we?"

"That's for sure."

"And," he said softly, "hopefully, they won't be the last."

I should've been prepared for what came next. He glanced at me and said, "You'll be in my prayers, Holly-Heart. I want God's will for both of us, individually and otherwise."

It was sweet. A direct result of the conversation we'd had earlier.

"I'll be praying for you, too." It was a promise I would keep.

119

SEVENTEEN

We, the fabulous first runner-ups from Colorado, toured the Red, Blue, and Green rooms at the White House the next morning. Then came the East Room, where the president held press conferences, followed by the State Dining Room. We received special treatment from our state senator because of our newly acquired status. Hotshot show choir members that we were!

Somehow, he arranged for us to meet the Secretary of State, and later, we "accidentally" ran into the First Cat, who seemed rather purr-y about being made over by so many doting teenagers. I almost took a picture of the perfectly groomed kitty to show to my ordinary fluff ball back home, but I remembered Sean's advice about flash photography and refrained.

Overhead were enormous crystal-laden chandeliers—one of the things that really grabbed me about this place. And the wide, wood molding around the fireplaces, doors, and windows. Maybe I was beginning to change my taste—old, historic things really were cool.

The Oval Office—the president's office in the west wing—was off-limits to the tour, of course, as were the First Family's private quarters upstairs. I was curious about what those rooms looked like, but having seen as much as I had here on the tour, my imagination took over. I decided the very next time *20/20* ran a special on the White House, I would tune in.

Overall, my assessment of the magnificent mansion was that it was old. Very old. Two hundred years old, to be exact.

"So, what did you think?" I asked Andie as we made our way outside afterwards.

"Too stuffy. A house oughta be a place to relax."

I smiled at her reaction. "Where you can put your feet up and not worry about it, right?" I thought of my dad's elegant beach house in southern California. Now there was a study in serious interior design. But that was Daddy's ... and Saundra's style.

"Do you miss Sean?" she asked later, as we headed for Capitol Hill.

"He just left, for pete's sake." I purposely evaded the question.

"Well, I have a feeling you'll be seeing him again." She tilted her curly head.

"He's really very special."

"No kidding," Paula piped up.

"Hey, whoa—don't forget about that dating book," Kayla urged.

I grinned. "Sean's planning to read it."

Andie clutched her throat. "Oh, no, it *is* serious!"

We joked around about it, but underlying all of our talk was a sense of doing what was right. We were growing up, trying on new ideas—eager to follow what the Bible said. Yep, we were nearing the end of our freshman year, all right, more mature than ever. But we were far from the end of our coming-of-age.

Next year, and the next, we would attempt to keep our eyes on Jesus, the ultimate grown-up and best example. And, in years to come, we would tell our own children about how we'd tripped and fallen, but gotten back up and plugged ahead.

❤   ❤   ❤

Late Wednesday afternoon, we arrived in Dressel Hills, tired but perfectly elated about the outcome of our trip. Mrs. Duncan couldn't stop talking about how wonderful we were—musically and otherwise.

"I think she's secretly hoping for a chance at Vienna," Andie said as we waited at the baggage claim area.

Jared had overheard. "How could that ever happen?"

"Let her dream," I answered. "She deserves it."

"Yeah. Some people deserve it more than others." And he was off to grab his bags, leaving us girls to wonder what he meant.

"That Jared," Andie said as we pulled each other's luggage off the conveyor, "does he ever say what he means?"

"He used to," I chimed in. "And, personally, I'm glad those days are over!"

Andie caught my eye. "You and me both."

❤ ❤ ❤

It wasn't long before Uncle Jack, Carrie, and Stephie showed up. The girls squeezed in hard against me as my stepdad gave me a hug.

"We missed you, Holly," Carrie said.

"We sure did!" Stephie remarked. "Miss Hibbard was . . ."

She stopped when her dad shook his head. "Our neighbor did her best," was all he said.

Carrie scrunched up her nose, and I figured there'd been some conflicts. Maybe with Stan. Of course, I was smart enough not to ask.

We headed for the automatic doors and to the parking lot.

"Someone's at home, waiting to see you," Uncle Jack said as he loaded my suitcases into the back of the van.

"I can't wait."

Stephie grabbed my hand. "Oh, Holly, our baby's so-o pretty!"

"Does she look like you?" I asked.

"Almost exactly," Carrie said. "And Stephie doesn't mind not being the baby of the family anymore."

"I never said that!" wailed Stephie.

I winked at her, letting her push in beside me on the van's second seat. "These things take time," I whispered in her ear, and she leaned her head against my arm.

Carrie crawled up front, riding shotgun with Uncle Jack. "You just wait till you hold April," she said, smiling back at me.

"She's all cuddly and sweet," my stepdad said. "But then, so were all of you at that age."

"And we're not *now?*" Carrie demanded.

He reached over and swished her long ponytail. "Now you're cuddly and ... and ... sometimes a little sour." It was just a joke, and Carrie loved it. We all did. Uncle Jack was cool.

The biggest surprise came when I walked into the house. There, on the Boston rocker, sat Stan—holding April.

I couldn't help it. I stared. Probably longer than I should've. "Wow, this is going to take some getting used to."

"So get over it," he muttered back at me.

"Hey, I think I must've missed something." I knelt down beside Stan and touched the tiny hand sticking out of the blanketed bundle.

"You missed everything," Stan said quietly. "But it made all the difference."

The guys in my life—when would they ever start saying what they meant?

"Are you telling me you're glad I went to Washington? That you wouldn't have fallen in love with your baby sister if I hadn't?"

He tried to conceal the smile. "Don't get smug," he said. "Wanna hold her?"

"What do you think?"

He stood up and let me sit in Mom's rocker, then placed my sister gently in my arms. "Oh, April," I cooed down into the precious, tiny face. "I'm so glad to meet you."

"We changed her name," Stan said flatly.

"How come?" I asked, shocked.

"She didn't exactly look like an April," he said.

I couldn't tell if he was serious or not. "Well, she does to me," I replied.

Carrie was giggling now. "Our baby has a nickname," she chanted. "Can you believe it?"

That figured. Uncle Jack was the master-giver of weird and wacky names.

"I almost hate to ask," I said.

Mom came downstairs just then, looking perky in her prettiest bathrobe. "Welcome home, honey."

"Did you honestly change April's name?" I asked as she kissed the top of my head.

She headed for the couch and Uncle Jack. "Modified it, I guess you'd say."

"To what?"

"April-Love," Stan said at last. "Because she reminds Mom of you."

"Oh, really?" I studied the rosebud face. "Maybe it's the shape of her chin."

"I thought you said she looked like *me!*" Stephie insisted.

Uncle Jack put his arm around Mom and they

snuggled, admiring their first child together—now asleep in my arms. "April is a combination of all of us." And my stepdad went right down the line. "She has her mother's eyes . . . and my good nature."

We laughed, then settled down for the rest of his comments.

"She has Stan's determination, Phil's smarts, and Mark's appetite."

"Poor kid," whispered Carrie.

"Now, hold on a minute," Uncle Jack said. He looked at Mom and gave her a peck on the end of her nose. "The baby has Stephie's dimples, Carrie's little nose, and Holly's . . ." He stopped, adding to the suspense. "She has Holly's good heart—and that's all there is to it."

I made the chair rock gently and felt the first, sweet stirrings of tiny April. Here we all were together. The people who mattered most in my life . . . and this new little one.

"By the way, Stan," I said, looking up, "thanks for what you did . . . about getting me to go."

"It was nothing," came the reply.

"Well, thanks anyway," I repeated.

"Hey . . . whatever." Stan was much too cool to show his true feelings, this brousin of mine. But maybe, just maybe, April-Love would help him with that macho stuff. From what I'd seen, it was already beginning to happen.

"Congratulations," Mom said about show choir. "Wish we could've heard you sing."

"Oh, you will," I told her. "Mrs. Duncan has some big plans for us ... media coverage, the works. Dressel Hills hasn't heard the end of us yet."

We sat there, taking turns talking. Later, Uncle Jack decided to have a short devotional. While he read from the Bible, I watched April's wee face, noting the family marks. The set and color of Mom's eyes, Carrie's nose, and Stephie's demure dimples ... but most of all, God's blessing.

Someday, I decided, if it was God's will, I would have a husband and a family. Maybe it was a girl thing to be thinking like this. Or simply a direct result of having had a fabulous weekend with Sean. Whatever it was, it was a good thing. And right.

That night a big, white moon shone brightly through my window as I looked out over the mountains of the Continental Divide. I remembered watching for Santa's elves to tiptoe over those mountains when I was a little girl. Of course, I was way beyond that now—too grown-up to believe in such childish things. I had better things to believe in. *Someone* to believe in. A Savior and friend—Jesus Christ.

When I slept in my own soft, canopy bed, I dreamed I could hear the angels whispering, "Holly-Heart" to me outside my window. And in their heavenly voices I heard the excitement of tomorrow—my future. The future that my all-wise heavenly Father lovingly held in his hands.

And in my sleep, I felt a flurry of joy.

❤ **About the Author** ❤

Beverly Lewis remembers well her baby-sitting years and being drawn to toddlers and children. Even as a young girl of ten or so, she liked to visit the nursery and hold the babies at her father's church in Lancaster, Pennsylvania.

To this day, she gets choked up over a newborn. But having raised three beautiful children from infancy to adolescence, Beverly's content with the adopted children the Lord has given to her and her husband. "I do think ahead to becoming a grand-mother . . . someday," she says with a smile. "But in the meantime, creating story characters—giving life to fictional people—keeps me very busy."

Remember: If you write to Beverly, always include a self-addressed, stamped envelope if you wish to receive a reply. Thanks!

Beverly Lewis
Author Relations
Zondervan Publishing House
Grand Rapids, MI 49530